POTIONS AND PLAYING CARDS

A Spooky Games Club Mystery Book 3

AMY MCNULTY

Crimson Fox
PUBLISHING

 Created with Vellum

Chapter One

"Four of hearts?" Fauna Vadas, pigtailed five-year-old werewolf in a pink overall dress, leaned over the small collection of cards she held before her and peered at her older sister with all the seriousness of a detective investigating a suspect.

Seven-year-old Flora tossed her thick, curly, dark brown hair over her shoulder. Jutting her chin up, she held her cards before her with the elegance of a lady cradling a porcelain cup of tea. "Go fish."

Fauna scowled and reached for a new card in the middle of the table, tucking whatever it was into her pile.

"Fish, fish, fish!" said three-year-old Falcon, running around the table and making puttering sounds like an old-fashioned airplane. His arms straight out to both sides, his airplane morphed into a flying fish as he started smacking his lips together to imitate bubble sounds.

His arm clipped the back of Flora's head and she shouted, "*Owwwww!*" as if her brother's errant hand had been a rock.

Falcon giggled, his curly, brown hair dancing across his dark eyes as he spun and spun, hitting his sister's back each time.

"*Dad!*" she said, tossing her cards face-down on the kitchen table in front of her.

"That's enough, Falcon. No hitting your sister. And we run outside, not indoors." Grady put his own cards down and stuck his pockmarked arm out to stop his son from smacking his daughter once more. I winced at the sight of the mottled dark flesh, as I'd managed to reattach his arm a couple of months back—having a blood mad werewolf for a toddler under a vampire's spell can lead to some pretty grim accidents—but I hadn't managed to erase all traces of the incident. My enchantments were improving even just two months later because I'd made a concerted effort to strengthen my magic. But I couldn't be sure I could have healed him any better today.

Falcon didn't let his dad's firm arm deter him from smacking a sister. Since Flora was out of reach, he giggled and spun right behind his dad to go hit little Fauna.

"That's enough!" Faine, my best friend, didn't often get angry, so even the slightest bit of firmness in her tone was enough to make the entire room grow quiet. Her children and husband stared at her, all echoes of one another. Grady was thin and tall, his lankiness passed on to his eldest daughter. Fauna seemed destined to take more after her petite mother, a full two heads shorter than her older sister. The kids' medium brown complexion was a couple of shades lighter than their father's, several shades darker than their fair-skinned mother. But both mother and father were evident in the kids' almost identical, angular features. Must have been the wolf genes in them all.

Falcon stared up at his mom, his eyes welling up with tears.

Faine was already starting to crack. "Oh, come on now, darling. You can't hit your sisters. You know that."

Flora let an exaggerated breath escape her lips and picked up her cards again. "Six of diamonds?" she asked her dad, pointedly ignoring her brother getting into trouble.

Grady grinned broadly and picked up his own pile, sliding a card across the table to his first born. "It's all yours."

Falcon was bawling now, and Faine bent down, the silk of her bold, green 1940s-style housedress swishing as she lifted her son into her arms. She whispered to him, her bright red mouth in a firm line, and Falcon cut short the waterworks, taking hold of one of his mom's chestnut ringlets dropping down from her broad, silk headband.

"Go fish!" shouted Fauna just as the potato I'd been peeling slipped from my hands, clunking down into the sink.

This time, everyone's eyes turned my way, to the sight of the local witch at their kitchen sink, a peeler in one hand.

"Sorry." I lifted the half-peeled potato apologetically. "NAELC," I said to the potato to clean it of anything it had picked up in the sink.

Then I went back to peeling by hand.

Every single day, sometime while the sun was overhead, I had to complete a good deed for someone in Luna Lane. Despite having the ability to cast enchantments, I had to complete the good deed with my own two hands. A little enchantment here and there to help me along—like cleaning a potato I'd already washed by hand—seemed to go unnoticed by the curse placed upon me before I'd been born. But it was a delicate balance. If I'd used my magic to peel the potatoes or just, with a wave of my arms, transformed the stack of potatoes into a giant, peeled pile in seconds—which I was fully capable of doing—it wouldn't count. If I didn't put some elbow grease into the task, when the sun went down, I'd have another silver stone scale somewhere on my body, most likely my left arm, until I ran out of space there entirely.

Peeling the potato, I glanced down at the "tattoo

sleeve" decorating my left arm, starting at my shoulder in a wrapping, weaving pattern all the way down to the back of my hand. The smaller scales were from my younger years, when my mom had been around to mitigate the effects of the curse and make sure I completed a good deed daily almost without fail. The larger ones had popped up in the past few months. Mom had been gone ten years now, and on the days I missed the good deed, the scales were growing bigger and bigger, as if to make up for lost time. I was already thirty, and surely, the wicked witch who had wished this upon me had expected me to turn to stone entirely long before now.

The pitter patter of little feet indicated Falcon had been put down and was running over to me.

"No running inside," Grady said sternly.

Falcon practically tripped stopping himself as he came around the kitchen island. He tugged on the bottom of my black dress skirt. "I can't help?" he asked. "Your witch curse?"

Adding the fully peeled potato to my growing stack, I *booped* his nose with a slimy potato-residue-covered finger and he giggled, wrinkling his brow. "That's right. I have to do this alone. But thank you. You're such a good helper!"

Faine shuffled into the kitchen behind her son as the rest of the family's game went wild. Someone seemed to have won. "You can help Mommy," she said, heading to the stovetop. She handed him a corncob. "Can you peel off these husks?"

Falcon grinned. He knew what came next after peeling off cornhusks.

While no one could help me accomplish my good deed, Faine was usually good at coming up with something I could do alone that would ease her burden of cooking countless meals a day from scratch while still leaving herself plenty to do so I wouldn't be stuck alone in her kitchen. Only today, the Vadases' café, Hungry Like a Pup, was closed. Faine and Grady believed in keeping the café open on Thanksgiving to open up the celebration to anyone in town who didn't want to be alone or make the big Thanksgiving meal at home. So the Sunday beforehand, they closed their café and made a meal just for the family at home.

Well, just for the family and me.

"You are *family,"* Faine had told me the year my mom had died, the first year I'd otherwise have been alone. That was before she'd gotten married herself, so it had just been the two of us. Her own parents had moved back to their werewolf home-town village by then. Soon enough, she'd met her fellow werewolf match from that same village and her family had grown, but I was still here every year, doing my part to help Faine with early-Thanks-giving dinner.

It took only a single crinkle, Falcon's chubby toddler fingers just barely peeling off the first husk.

Her senses somehow activated—I'd guess it was her sense of smell, if cornhusks had a scent and if she had a nose—Broomhilde, my companion and enchanted broomstick, lifted her brush from the pillow she'd curled up on near the crackling fire. Shaking her bristles, she soared over the game table to the shrieks and delights of the girls and stretched out her body fully in front of little Falcon, eager for a treat.

Practically gasping for air as he danced in place with delight, Falcon handed Broomie the cornhusk in his hand and she slurped it up, the shaking of her bristles like munching as she ate the only sustenance she could—or at least the only food-like thing she expressed any interest in. She'd lived nine lives already as different cats before becoming my broomstick, but she'd lost her carnivorous tastes entirely as a witch's broomstick.

"I want to feed her!" said Flora, popping up around the other side of the island.

"Me too!" added Fauna. She had to pull out and then climb up on a stool across from me to see inside the kitchen.

The stovetop fan whirred and Faine blew out a breath to shift aside a curl that had escaped her headband to dangle over her deep brown eyes. "Okay, take the corn—everyone head to the backyard and play out there! Dinner won't be ready for another hour or so." As if that reminded her, she quickly peeked into one of the dual-stacked ovens she had going and nodded, seemingly satisfied with what she found in there.

The kids broke into squeals as Falcon led Broomie to the sliding glass door, the broomstick stretched stiff and locked on the cornhusk in his hand like a hound. The girls darted in the kitchen to collect the rest of the corncobs and Grady slipped in behind them to plant a kiss on his wife's temple. "You sure you have this all handled?"

"Of course," Faine said brightly. "I have Dahlia." Fauna wove between her parents to head for the fridge and grab a juice box, practically knocking her mom out of the way. "Though letting the kids tire themselves out by running around outside might help some?"

Grady laughed and put his hands on Fauna's shoulders, directing her to the yard, where her brother and sister were already playing.

A blast of chilly air entered the house as Grady scrambled to gather a collection of kids' coats out of the mudroom closet. "Hey! It's cold out!"

Luckily, werewolves seemed to handle the cold better than most. Warmer body temperatures, maybe.

I was not so lucky. Shivering, I wished I'd kept my knitted shawl on, though that was quickly solved once Grady had gone outside and pulled the sliding door shut behind him.

Faine hummed, the tune almost drowned out by the whirring fan.

I put the last potato on the top of my pile, one among at least three dozen. "Finished," I said, flexing my hand as I set the peeler down.

Faine turned to me and smiled. "Thank you for your help, Dahlia."

Like a tide come in to wash away etchings in the sand, I felt a sense of relief flood my body, an almost tangible release of tension. At the underside of my wrist, a tingling patch of skin cooled down. I wondered if I slipped up one of these days if that was where the next stone scale would be. It'd be the first one on the inside of my arm. Eventually, my arm might grow too covered—too heavy—for any kind of movement.

"What's wrong?" Faine set the pots on the stove to simmer and turned off the fan.

"Nothing." I tried fluffing her off. I thought of something I could use to shift the focus away from me, something I'd meant to do today anyway. I reached into the pouch attached to the golden belt around my waist and pulled out a stack of cash. I'd summoned it from the space between dimensions Mom had stored it all in for us before her move to Luna Lane. I counted it out. It numbered in the hundreds. "I'm finally remembering to pay off my Hungry Like a Pup tab," I said. "With tip. Happy Early Thanksgiving."

Faine *tsked* me and put her hand around mine, bending my fingers over the cash. "You know I don't care about that. With all the work you do around town, we like to take care of you."

"Don't be ridiculous." I shoved it into her hand. "I owe you, and I don't need it—the house is paid off and Mayor Abdel hasn't raised our property taxes in twenty years. Of course I want the money to help my friends rather than just sit there where nobody can reach it."

Faine frowned. She knew about Mom's seemingly endless supply of cash. I actually didn't even know when it'd run out—if it ever would. I'd cross that bridge when it came to it. Like Faine said, Luna Lane would take care of me.

But Faine had outside suppliers to pay, kids to outfit with the latest clothes and toys…

"Thank you," said Faine simply. She took off two bills and handed them back to me. "But this tip is preposterous. Take some of it back."

I pushed her hand gently back toward her. "I want you to have it."

She bypassed my hand and tucked the money straight into my still-open pouch, buttoning the clasp closed. "Then save it for the next time you pay off your tab."

I grumbled but didn't put up more of a fight, crossing my arms sourly.

"Okay, so now that we're done with that *distraction*, albeit a kindly intended one," she said, "tell me what's wrong."

I hadn't fooled her at all. "I... I really want to break this curse, Faine."

She put an arm around me and guided me to the other side of the kitchen island, pulling out a stool and sitting on it before indicating the one Fauna had left out. "Do you want to talk about it?"

What was there left to say?

Still... Sometimes it helped just to vent.

"My mom wasn't able to stop it," I said, taking the offered seat and threading my fingers together on the counter. "And she was a more powerful witch than I am."

Faine knew all of this but listened intently anyway. Because she was just that kind of person. She could put even the snootiest ghost, the most sullen vampire at ease.

My thoughts reminded me with a sharp pain of Ginny Kincaid, wherever her spirit now was.

She'd still had regrets that might tie her to this realm even after she'd had her revenge on the ones who'd killed her... But I hadn't seen her in weeks. No one had.

"And you've tried a lot of the potions in your book," said Faine.

"Not *every* potion." I twirled a lock of my long, wavy, fiery-red hair around an elongated finger nervously. "And I stopped brewing something new every day."

"Because you were becoming too obsessed with it,"

said Faine. She stuck a dainty finger in the cream she'd set out on the island earlier and licked it off her pinky. "It's better to face each day one at a time. Complete your good deed, stave away the new scale for the day, and *then* you have time for experimentation."

My shoulders sinking, I leaned on my elbows, my palms cradling my cheeks. "Or just pretend I don't have a curse hanging overhead."

"You can't experiment *every day*," she said, nudging the bowl toward me. "You have to relax, too."

"Yeah." I dug my own finger into the cream and placed it to my lips. Sweet, but also just the right amount of tart. I dipped another finger in.

"All right. I better put that in the fridge before any other little fingers get dunked in there." Laughing, Faine stole the bowl of cream from me so there'd be some for the pumpkin pie.

She headed for the kitchen table, where the cards were still spread out across the surface, and started cleaning up. It was almost an instinct with her, both at home and at her café.

"Say, speaking of relaxing, what about a night of cards with Games Club?" Faine held the double deck in her hand and wriggled her eyebrows.

"If we play anything other than Go Fish, you'll have to teach me." Luna Lane's Spooky Games Club was still meeting every Saturday, despite the not one, but *two* horrible incidents involving murder that clouded the club in my mind. But I had to admit, the more frequently we met, the more it was growing on me.

I didn't win much, though—and if we took up cards, I knew Faine was going to wipe the floor with me.

"Euchre," said Faine succinctly, as if that were the end of that. "Euchre would be perfect—*oh, oh, oh!*"

"What?" My back stiffened, and I whirled around, my arms out and ready to enchant whatever was attacking her.

Faine paled and then chuckled, her cheeks reddening. "Sorry. I just had an idea."

"An idea?" I lowered my arms.

The doorbell rang, and Faine's eyes sparkled mischievously as she slunk by me to get it. "They're early."

"Who's—" But she didn't give me a chance to ask.

"Come in! Come in!" Faine's voice carried out from the mudroom and I followed her to the door.

In shuffled Milton Woodward, his back hunched, his wiry, white hair sticking up in every direction, though he seemed to have made an effort to dress up today. When Faine took his coat, he revealed not only his late wife's reading glasses on a chain around his neck—he didn't need them, but he wore them to remind him of her—but also a red, checkered bowtie atop a button-up long-sleeved shirt and a pair of clean-pressed khakis that could have been purloined from his adult nephew's closet.

And speaking of, Cable Woodward stepped in behind his elderly uncle, shaking out his short, dark, wavy hair. Snowflakes peppered throughout his tresses were melting, along with my heart at the sight of his broad grin beneath those circular wire-rimmed glasses.

I had to shake my head for my brain to even catch up with me after locking my green eyes with Cable's dark ones. Faine took his wool coat, revealing the tall, strapping, muscular form that popped against his own button-up shirt, silk red tie, and khakis. He was like a romance novel's idea of a professor on sabbatical, which he was—an American literature professor who taught in Scotland. He was just here for the rest of the semester. That meant his stay was at least half over, if not more.

You can't leave Luna Lane. You can't leave Luna Lane, I repeated like a mantra in my head. I really couldn't. The curse kept me here. Otherwise, I might have been out there doing good deeds with more significance than washing windows and peeling potatoes.

After hanging up their coats next to my shawl and black witch's hat with the purple band, Faine wrapped her arm around Milton's and led him at a slow pace to the dining table. "Watch your step. It's slippery out today, huh?"

"Like an ice rink." Milton cackled, then stared at Faine. "Frieda?"

That was Faine's mom's name. They looked a little alike, but Frieda had never had Faine's eclectic fashion sense.

"It's Faine, Milton. Frieda's daughter. Frieda left the café to me and went home with my dad."

"Home...?" Milton looked around. "Frieda and Jonathan's house."

"Yes, this is their house." Faine patted his hand and escorted him to the table, not bothering to correct him or otherwise elaborate. Milton's memories often dwelled on the past.

"So I take it you didn't know we'd be here?" Cable had his glasses off now and had pulled an eyeglass rag out of his pocket. He ran it over his lenses to clean them of the water droplets.

"No." I exchanged a look with Faine across the room really fast and she snickered as she headed into the kitchen. I turned back to Cable, who was putting his glasses back on. "But that doesn't mean you're not a welcome surprise."

"When I found out Hungry Like a Pup was going to be closed today, I was just going to cook for Uncle Milton and me, but Faine insisted we join them. She might have told me I could find you here, too." He tugged at his collar and if the crisp, cold air weren't lingering so much in the doorway, I would have found myself flushing.

"You have perfect timing," said Faine from the kitchen, her voice loud enough to carry over the fan she'd turned back on. "Because an idea just struck me moments before you walked in. Spooky Games Club should host a euchre tournament!"

We should… what?

Was that the idea that had struck her as she'd cleaned off the table, scaring me to death?

Outside, one of the kids was howling. It was, once again, nearing the full moon—and thankfully, we'd found out last month that the werewolves' exposure to para-paranormal had not lasted long enough to impede their transformation at all.

Beyond the sliding glass door, little Falcon was crouched like a dog and jumping up to bite at the snowflakes that fell. Though the ground was still slightly too warm for the snow to last, the kids—and Broomie—were zipping all around, trying to catch flakes on their tongues and bristles, respectively.

"Euchre?" Milton nodded. "Leana loves euchre. Don't bet against her team." He cackled as he patted the kitchen table and reached for the tall stack of cards. Sometimes he forgot his wife had passed on.

Cable frowned, pinning his arms tightly across his stomach. "Sounds great," he said. "But if we can't manage to put it all together before this upcoming weekend, I won't be here to help with it."

A sudden and terrible weight grew heavy in my chest.

Chapter Two

"*What* do you mean, you won't be here this weekend?" Faine clanked a wooden spoon against her bubbling pot and slipped the cover back on before turning around to inspect Cable. "Your sabbatical is for the whole semester, isn't it?"

Right? He was supposed to have at least one more month in Luna Lane. Maybe two.

And then... *Then* I could prepare to let him go. He could visit his uncle from time to time, but I'd have to let him go.

What was I even thinking? As if he were mine to let go to begin with.

Letting out a long breath, Cable joined his uncle at the table. "Well, I talked to the head of my department, and he's pleased with my research so far." I knew he spent most of his days poring over books and writing up a thesis of some kind—when he wasn't playing games with Club or otherwise assisting me in solving murders. But, hopefully, we'd seen the last of those. "But he figures as long as I'm in America, I should go to places of historical literary significance. Get a closer look at some original documents, get some pretty pictures for a presentation." He seemed to be staring directly across at Faine, almost too fixatedly, as if he didn't want to look at me at all as I neared.

"Well, that might be fun," said Faine, gathering the peeled potatoes and dropping them bit by bit into a boiling pot of water she had ready on the stove. "Where are you off to?"

My throat was suddenly so dry. I found myself reaching for the stool at the breakfast bar just to steady my wobbly knees. What was wrong with me?

"I haven't decided yet," he said simply. "The Langston Hughes House in Harlem, Amherst College in Massachusetts, the Mark Twain Boyhood Museum in Hannibal, Missouri... I can just get in my car and go. That's the beauty of a wide open country like this one."

Wide and open. Getting in his car and going. I fumbled now, slipping onto the stool. Faine noticed right away and her friendly smile cracked as she looked at me over the stack of remaining potatoes. "But will you be back?" she asked. I couldn't voice the question myself, couldn't pretend to be excited for him.

"Yes," said Cable, making his way over to us.

The vise squeezing my heart let up.

"I don't plan to be gone longer than a couple of weeks—then I'll come back and finish up my research paper here." He surveyed the counter, his gaze zeroing in on the pile of potato peels. "Need any help?"

"Don't be silly," said Faine. "You're my guest."

Cable finally seemed to notice I was there. "Did you do your good deed?"

"Yes," I said, running my hand over my left arm almost as a reflex. "So that means I can use some enchantments to help. YDIT." Waving both arms over the island, the potato peels started to make their way to the garbage can for compost in the corner, the lid lifting automatically to greet the new additions. The lid wasn't me, though. It was battery-operated.

With a yelp, Faine jumped in to snatch the last of the peeled potatoes midair before I threw them out, too.

"Sorry," I mumbled, clasping my hands together and jamming them down between my legs. My shoulders slouched as I felt about ready to sink into the vinyl covering the stool.

Cable offered me a sly grin. "Maybe your magic is growing too strong now. You almost enchanted away the pie." He leaned over the cooling pumpkin pie and inhaled in deeply. "I might have panicked."

Tucking a long strand of hair behind my ear, I tried my best to smile, but my throat was still constricted. You'd have thought he'd have told us he'd never set foot in Luna Lane again the way my heart was thundering on.

"Dahlia Poplar can never be too strong a witch," said Faine, stirring the potatoes in the bubbling water. "Not since she's going to break her curse someday." She seemed so much more confident of that than I was.

"Of course." Cable focused on a big speck of black on the Formica. "I didn't mean anything. If you could…" He stopped himself.

"If I could what?" I asked, finding my voice.

"If you could leave town, I would have—"

"Ack!" Milton's scream drew all of our attention. "There's a flying broom outside!" He jumped to his feet, practically tripping over the chair.

Today he must not have remembered about Luna Lane's paranormal residents—specifically its red-haired witch.

"Uncle, Uncle, it's fine." Cable moved in to soothe him, pointing out the sliding glass door as Falcon, Fauna, and Flora alike jumped up to dangle off of Broomie's shaft, Flora's feet just barely scraping the ground, leaving her much-shorter siblings a good several feet off of it. Grady hovered nearby, his dark face ashen, as if ready to jump in and snatch a falling child at any minute.

"Broomie?" asked Milton, as if he suddenly remembered her.

"Yes, Broomhilde. Dahlia's broomstick." Cable

guided Milton back to the table, sliding the pile of cards toward him.

"That's a double deck," said Faine, scurrying around the kitchen. A little bit of gravy had somehow gotten on her cheek.

"Uncle Milton, why don't you split the decks? Make two piles. Don't put any of the same cards in the same pile." Cable started divvying up the cards for him.

I still wondered what, exactly, he'd been about to tell me.

"Cinnamon?" asked Milton, studying me. "Broomhannah?" he said, looking outside again.

My mom and her companion broomstick. We looked enough alike, my mom and me, that the confusion made a lot of sense.

"The witch of Luna Lane," I said, winking as I put my hands on my hips.

"Yes, yes," said Milton, focusing on the cards, taking a portion of the stack out of Cable's hands.

"Do we need to increase our visitation schedule, do you think, while you're gone?" Faine asked, still buzzing around the kitchen like a bee with a dozen flowers from which to secure nectar. She was refer-ring to residents of the town taking turns checking in on Milton. It was what we'd done after Leana had died and before Cable had arrived. It was what we'd do again once Cable was gone for good.

"Oh, I can't believe I forgot." Cable shifted his glasses up his nose. "My mom is coming to town for

Thanksgiving—she said she'll stay as long as I'm gone, maybe longer. Spend some time with her brother."

"Your mom?" I hadn't seen Ingrid Woodward in years. She was always jetting off around the globe. She'd even schooled her son herself with the world as his classroom. She'd grown up in Luna Lane, but her son had never had roots to speak of—he'd only come here once before he'd shown up on Milton's doorstep this past September.

"Ingrid," said Milton, shaking a bony, gnarled finger in Cable's direction. "You're Ingrid's boy."

"That's right, Uncle." Cable handed him the rest of the stack of cards.

"She can play euchre, too," said Milton, busying himself with the stacks.

"Well, there you go. My mom can help with the tournament," said Cable.

"Wait, are we doing this?" I asked.

But my comment went ignored.

"Nonsense," said Faine. "Spooky Games Club can't sponsor a playing card tournament without one of its second generation founding members."

Cable fiddled with his shirtsleeves as he watched his uncle sort the cards. There was a hint of pink to his ears. "Well, she'll be here tomorrow, so we have a few days—"

"Tuesday, then!" said Faine, clapping her hands together.

"Faine, that's a lot of planning to do in just two

days." I waved around at the several food stations she currently had going. "And you always outdo yourself for the town celebration on Thanksgiving."

"The full moon," added Milton, suddenly astoundingly lucid.

"Right," I said. "The full moon is Thanksgiving eve, too. You're going to exhaust yourself."

"Why don't I do most of the planning?" offered Cable.

I looked him over. "What about planning for your trip? And your research?"

"I'm taking the week off," he said. "For the holiday. And as for the trip... I'm just going to start driving in one of those directions I had in mind and see where my wheels take me."

Must have been nice to be so free.

A buzzer went off and Faine rushed to grab some mitts before heading over to open the oven. "Perfect!" she said, bringing out the turkey with steady hands and careful steps. It was so large, it practically outsized my diminutive friend.

The sliding glass door opened and the children's laughter grew louder inside the home.

Grady poked his head in. "Do I smell turkey?" That was a canine for you.

"Yes, you smell turkey," said Faine with a smile. "Now get the kids washed up."

Grady said his *hello*s to Cable and Milton before getting barreled over by the kids.

It was a hectic next ten minutes or so that felt

23

like several hours, considering how much Faine got done—without once asking for my magic to make things easier—but soon enough, the extra table leaves had been brought out, Broomie was snoring on a pillow in front of the fire, drying off her bristles, and the rest of us were gathered around a feast that had the canine members of the party literally salivating.

Falcon reached out toward a leg of the turkey and Flora smacked his hand.

"Ow. No hitting," said Falcon, cradling his hand against his chest.

"That's right," said Faine. She narrowed her eyes at Flora for a moment but then smiled. "But your sister is right. First we have to say our thanks."

"Me! Me!" Fauna snatched hold of her opposite arm, as if she could somehow boost it to go higher.

We all laughed. "Go ahead," said Grady.

"I am thankful for Mommy and Daddy and Flora and Falcon… and Broomie and Auntie Dahlia and… and…" She looked to Cable and Milton, as if suddenly remembering she'd never paid them much attention before.

"Uncle Milton and Uncle Cable," said Faine for her. "Very lovely, Fauna. Thank you."

"I'm thankful!" said Falcon, raising his hand in imitation of his sister, who'd gotten all those laughs. "I'm thankful for that! And food!"

"I am thankful for my family and friends and doing well in school," said Flora, her hands clasped together in front of her as if in prayer. "Which still stinks."

Grady nudged her. "I am thankful for such wonderful children," said Grady. His gaze turned on Faine, and you could feel the love melting his expression even further. "And a gorgeous wife who does so much for our family." As if remembering the rest of us were here, he smiled cheekily and looked away. "And friends here to join us, making the day an even merrier one!"

"I am thankful for the most wonderful children, husband, and friends." Faine stared at her husband of almost a decade. "I really couldn't do anything without you."

Cable sniffled and I was surprised to see him shifting his glasses and dabbing a tear out of the corner of his eye.

He noticed us staring at him.

"Sorry," he said, his shoulders sinking. "I always cry at weddings."

That made the rest of the adults present crack up.

"I'm thankful for family," Cable said, taking it all in stride as he gripped his uncle by the hand, "and new friends." He looked at each of us in turn, and I may have been imagining it, but I thought his eyes lingered on me the longest.

"Me, too," said Milton, though none of us were *new* friends to him, not really.

Now it was my turn.

I opened my mouth, and it went dry for a moment. But Falcon's puppy-like whining drove me back. The kids were getting hungry, the food cold.

"I'm thankful for cherished friends," I said. "And for a place like Luna Lane to call home." I raised the glass of wine Faine had poured for all the adults. Everyone followed suit.

"Here, here," said Cable, though he of all people agreeing that Luna Lane was home made a heaviness grow in my limbs, the glass of wine almost too much to hold up.

I sipped it carefully, being sure not to overdo it, remembering vaguely how I'd embarrassed myself drinking a few extra margaritas last month to screw up my courage for the enchantment I'd been about to undertake.

As everyone dug in, the warm conversation devolving into the buzzing of bees in my mind, I cradled the cool, smooth stem of my glass and stared at Cable across the table from me. His upcoming trip may be for just a short while, but he was leaving soon enough.

I had a month or two at most to lift my curse, or I could basically count on never seeing him again.

Chapter Three

*A*s if to drive home the urgency of my dilemma, I decided to try stepping foot outside of Luna Lane, beyond the invisible barrier that kept me from reaching the world beyond the woods.

I'd already flown this entire barrier all around town. It encased me in a circle. On the singular road out of town, I knew right where my access to the world cut off. And here, I knew where the barrier stood several miles to the north of that road. There were markers that had imprinted on me. Even if I hadn't stood here, I could close my eyes and picture it vividly.

The bent branch on this old, scarred tree to the right of me.

The moss-covered stone to the left, now half covered in fallen leaves.

All so close to the little lake, to the site where

Eithne's cabin had once stood. All these years, and I hadn't known.

I'd been so focused on the world beyond that barrier, that enticing place beyond my reach, that I'd never examined what had been right at my feet.

Taking a deep breath, I reached a hand out. It glided through the air closer, closer…

And then my fingers bent, their progress impeded. I pushed on and my fingers curled into a fist. I drove that fist against the nothingness in front of me, but the wall I could not see may as well have been made of solid stone.

I let out a scream and banged against it. Hard. Harder. My fists grew sore.

Leaning against the solid nothingness, I laughed. If anyone came across me now, they'd see a defeated witch collapsed like a talented mime against nothing at all, her cheek squished, her shoulders slumped.

But it wasn't nothing at all to me.

With a chirrup, Broomie called me back over toward the lake.

We'd come here for reasons other than to let me mope.

Monday afternoon. Another day, another trip to the woods. A potion to deepen one's empathy. I didn't know how it might help me break my curse, but I was out of the more straightforward potential solutions. Page 332 of 781 potions in Mom's book. I'd managed to try a few in the past month, and there'd been some more falsely promising ones I'd tried ages ago. Then there were the ones for which ingredients were entirely too scarce for me to try.

But maybe Eithne Allaway, the wicked witch who'd cursed me before birth, had kept a few of the more stranger ingredients in her cabin in the woods surrounding Luna Lane. Maybe there were remnants to be uncovered.

I'd been back here several times in the weeks since discovering the wilted wreckage where Eithne's cabin had once stood. I'd tasked Ginny with examining it first, but we hadn't had a chance to talk about what she may have found—if anything —before she'd disappeared, perhaps moving on at last to her final resting place.

Because I'd had no such luck since in discovering anything useful beyond broken-up vials and the faded etchings of runes in what had once been the cabin floor.

Though the noises she made were confined to those an old-fashioned twig bristle broom could produce, Broomie practically whistled as she scraped away soggy leaves, moss, and dirt caked over the length of Eithne's cabin. She'd gotten used to our routine. If the day allowed for it, after completing a good deed, it was off to the woods, to Eithne's cabin, to see what else we could gather for future spells.

Though the answer to that was becoming more and more often "a whole lot of nothing."

The cabin hadn't been the biggest abode. I

didn't know how much more searching we could be doing.

As Broomie brushed aside a soggy pile, something glinted from within.

"Wait!" I shouted at her, practically throwing aside the plant life I'd gathered from the surrounding woods to get a better look.

Broomie stiffened, growing more alert as I skidded to my knees and dug away at the dirt.

The gritty dirt and mud caked under my nails as I got nearer and nearer to the thing…

Which turned out to be, if I was deducing this right, a shiny, holey candy wrapper. I made out the letters "aff" beneath the caked-on dirt.

"Those were good," someone said behind me. "I had a bit of a sweet tooth, I'd admit. Shame they stopped producing them in the '80s."

The woman's voice was deceptively kind, traces of an Irish lilt that somehow made my entire body feel hollowed out.

"Eithne." I spun around, landing on my rear in the soft mud, the candy wrapper flitting from my hand into the chilly breeze.

The lanky, lovely Eithne Allaway stood at what would have once been the threshold of her cabin, one hand holding up her black broomstick companion, which was as stiff as if it weren't alive at all.

My own broomstick companion was shaking, whimpering, behind my back at the sight of them.

I wished I could join her in hiding.

Eithne flicked her long, silver hair over the shoulder of her lilac dress, not even jostling the wide brim of her matching lilac witch's hat.

"You know, I have to love that the daily good deeds have trained you to act as if you were just some commonplace human," she said, her perfect button nose rising in the air. "Digging around in the dirt instead of just enchanting your object to you."

My mouth opened—I was scrambling for a retort. But she wasn't finished.

"Your mother had the same problem." With a flourish of her one free hand, Eithne, the powerful witch that she was, performed magic without even speaking her desire backward. "Too attached to the *mundane*. She almost forgot she wasn't one of them."

Around us, the leaves, the grass, the debris shifted.

"That was why her magic never rivaled mine."

The walls of the cabin reformed, building upward. Above us, the roof joined the walls, built from scraps of the lost cabin, from the surrounding woods, whatever was necessary to make her vision a reality.

"Don't—Don't talk about my mother," was all I managed to get out. My hand clutched Broomie's handle, as much to offer her support as to find some of my own.

Eithne laughed, an airy, spine-tingling sound. "Your mother wasn't the perfect angel you think she was."

I scrambled to my feet. Around us, the cabin—small, rustic—was complete, not a speck of dust out of place. In the fireplace hung a cast-iron cauldron, summoned up from the depths of the dirt below like some kind of long-buried treasure. A roaring fire crackled, and Eithne's black broomstick came to life, soaring to it. Though it curled up like a cat as Broomie might have under different circumstances, there was a sharpness to its angles, an alertness to its core, that made it seem more like a ploy to entice someone to pet it—only to snap the unsuspecting hand into its maw.

I blinked. I'd gone from investigating the ruins of a cabin to standing in it as if it had never been destroyed at all.

I spun to her potion table, so much like my own. The flasks were all empty, every last one.

"Looking for something in particular?" she crooned.

On shaky feet, I rose up, leaning on Broomie to stand. I realized we were standing in the center of Eithne's rune circle and quickly moved to exit it—

"YATS," she said, actually whipping both arms out in front of her, putting so much into this spell, I had no choice but to obey.

The runes lit up like a rapidly falling set of dominoes around me.

I was trapped. In my enemy's most potent place.

I'd curse my foolishness, but how could I have predicted... this?

You know she's been in town. Toying with you. Helping unleash chaos. Of course she could watch you walk right into her trap.

Broomie shook in my hand.

"If you want to kill me, just do it!" I snapped, sending a silent apology to my broomstick. When I died, she would, too.

"If I'd wanted to kill you, I would have done it already." Eithne examined her purple-painted nails from the other side of the rune circle.

"Do you think me turning to stone won't *kill* me?" I pointed out.

She arched an eyebrow. "You've managed to avoid growing scales on any place but your arm. What would *you* know about what will happen when it spreads to your body—to your head? What makes you so sure you'll die when you become fully stone? I happen to have it on good authority you'll stay conscious, immobile, a silent observer for all time."

The hairs on the nape of my neck prickled. I'd never even considered turning to stone anything but a death sentence.

"No." The sound was gurgled, coming from my throat.

"You can see for yourself if you'd like. Maybe bet it all on true love's kiss being able to break the spell." She laughed as she reached her potion table, lifting up one empty flask after another, as if searching for something.

True love's kiss? I'd never even considered such a thing. That was a solution from fairy tales.

Besides, what did I know about true love? I'd kissed my vampire ex, Draven, plenty of times, had even given my first one as a child to a pubescent Hitesh Mahajan behind his parents' shop one afternoon on a dare, and I was no closer to a cure for this curse than I had been the day I'd come into this world.

"Why?" I croaked. "Why do you hate me so much?"

"Darling, who said anything about hating you?" Eithne held one particular empty flask up to the sunlight streaming in through her sole window and nodded.

"My mother, then," I said. My heart was about to burst up through my throat. "You hated her enough to curse *me*, a child you hadn't even met yet, to kill—" I stopped. The flask she had in her hand. It didn't quite match the rest of them. There was a slight difference, a slight irregularity to the bulbous shape that made it seem far too familiar.

It was one of ours—Mom's and mine. And I'd seen it in her hand before, the day I'd come home to find my mother dead.

"Your mother turned my life upside down." Eithne whirled on her heel, a sharp flash of anger streaking over her violet eyes. She gestured around her with the empty flask. "I had a peaceful life here.

Quiet. Amusing." Her eyebrows arched, her usual serenity leaking back into her expression.

"You *asked* her to move here! You told me that yourself."

"Yes, well... One is allowed to at least have some regrets over one's own actions. Don't you feel the same?"

I bit my lip. I hadn't noticed Leana, my grandmother figure, suffering, hadn't imagined Ginny's real past—I'd even thought my magic responsible for injury and death for a time.

But those regrets weren't the same kind of thing.

"Then why did you wait so long to kill her?" I asked hoarsely, clutching Broomie tighter against my chest.

Instead of answering, Eithne looked at the empty flask in her grip and blew on it, her magic working again without words or funneling through her hands.

Inside appeared a potion, though it was only half-full. With a start, I saw the red substance and realized I'd seen it before—time and time again.

And not just, as I was only now remembering, the night I'd found Eithne standing over my mother's dead body, the flask in hand.

"Para-paranormal." I clutched at my throat. As cowed by her power as I was, I hadn't even *attempted* to use my own enchantments to break free of this trap. But now I knew I'd be entirely useless.

"Yes," said Eithne. "A mere illusion of a memory." She snapped her fingers and the vial was empty once more. "You saw me with it that night."

"My mother's death," I said. "It produced the para-paranormal you wanted. And you took it away. Was *that* it? That was why you killed her? You needed that?"

Eithne reached through the rune circle and held the empty flask out to me. I didn't want to do anything she wanted me to, but I took it numbly, my fingers caressing the smooth glass, as if I were somehow reaching through time and space to embrace my mother. "It takes two to produce para-paranormal, darling," she said. "You know that by now. Two acts of dark magic."

"You—" My tongue froze. "Who helped you? Who helped you kill her?"

"There were only two of us in the house." Eithne smiled. "The answer is right in front of you."

"No." My voice was more a croak than a whisper. "My mother couldn't have performed any dark magic with you. She wouldn't have. Her *death* triggered its creation. That means there was a third paranormal person—"

"Believe what you will. It matters little to me."

I smashed the empty flask to the ground, startling Broomie in my hand. "Liar!"

Eithne flicked one long finger and her broomstick came sauntering over to her, positioning itself between her legs and smoothly lifting her up in the air to sit on it like a practiced acrobatic routine.

"Dark magic is in your blood, little do-gooder witch. The cold, dark magic you find so distasteful."

"It was always in your blood. I should have told you." Mom's words rung loudly in my head. She'd even started to speak of something else—the cold, dark magic?

No. No, no, no. This made no sense.

"There's no such thing as a do-gooder witch," said Eithne. Above her, the cabin roof started disintegrating, the shingles and beams beginning to rot, returning to the soil in which it had been caked. "If you'd ever met another witch, you'd know that."

Tears stung my eyes, the headache I felt from keeping the dam from breaking searing in my head. "I know that. *You've* shown me that."

Eithne laughed as the cabin walls started decaying, the fire extinguishing with a hiss as the fireplace folded away, the cauldron retreating below. "I am not an exception. Your mother was. But she wasn't always that way."

Gritting my teeth, I dug my heels into the rune circle below me, even as the lights of the symbols faded, the wood broke away, and the weeds grew up and through. "Like I'd believe *you.*"

"Believe me or not, it won't help you with your curse. But maybe accepting what runs in your blood will." Her broomstick took off, flying up into the early evening sky and the blood orange of the horizon. The sky cracked as she met it, an echo of thunder ringing out despite the clear sky, the colder temperature.

My legs shook with relief, and I collapsed to the ground, the ruins of the cabin suddenly still and silent all around me.

Chapter Four

*M*y heart was hammering so loudly, I could barely hear anything over the thundering in my ears. I knew I was hardly in the best frame of mind to work enchantments, but I had to talk to my mom. No more dithering. Straight to the point.

She had to tell me what had happened that day —and she had to tell me where she'd come from, why she'd ever trusted Eithne to help her in the first place.

My glass flasks clicked and clanked as I sorted through the potions I'd previously brewed to find one that could give me a power boost.

Nothing.

And no ingredients to whip one up quickly, either.

Growling, I decided I'd try it without the help.

Broomie bent over limply, her bristles dragging

across the ground as she lay flat in front of my rune circle as if depressed. "I know. If I summon my mom too many times, I'll never be able to see her again. But what else can I do?" I snapped at her.

She bristled and shuffled away.

"Sorry," I called after her, but she was too sullen, too shook by our encounter. She scurried under the couch skirt with the flower design. "Broomie—I'm sorry."

She gave no response. I'd just need to give her space and time to sulk.

"I can do this." I shook my arms out, the left hand alarmingly not as limber as the right, the shiny stone scales laughing up at me. That was like a punch to the gut just as I was trying to give myself a pep talk.

No matter.

"RALPOP NOMANNIC, EMOC!" I said. "REHTOM YM, EMOC!"

Though I felt a surge of power channel down through my witch's hat, into my core, and out through my arms, though I saw the runes begin faintly to glow...

Nothing happened.

No mother in the midst of my rune circle. No bundle of cinnamon sticks and a branch from a poplar tree.

I screamed out the enchantment again.

Nothing.

"No, no, no..." I rubbed my left arm. It was

either me, the fact that I'd been too impatient to brew a power-boosting potion, or…

My mother's spirit could never be recalled from the realm beyond again.

Scrambling to the potion book, I flipped to the standard power-boosting ones, jolting to a stop as the inside of the cover caught my eye. The Poplar family crest, Mom had told me once. Square, shiny, and embossed in gold. At the center was a red circle, which reminded me startlingly of the jewel Virginia had had in her brooch, the one she'd told me Mom had given her *to keep her grounded*. I shook my head. I didn't know why that mattered now, especially with Virginia no longer around. But if I had a chance, I'd ask Mom.

First I'd need to restock the power boosters, make a bunch of them—

There was a knock at the door.

My heart jumped into my throat.

My first instinct was that it was Eithne—but when had she ever knocked?

If that wicked witch wanted to bother me more this evening, she would have just turned up behind me and breathed down my neck.

I yanked the door open.

Draven stood on the other side of it, his pallid hands tucked into the pockets of his leather pants.

It was night out. I hadn't even registered that.

Luckily, I'd helped Doc Day out this morning with some medical supply organization and ordering to complete my good deed—before I'd run into any wayward witches in the woods.

"Can I come in?" Draven asked after a long beat.

His long, blond hair shifted over the shoulder of his black leather jacket, open to reveal a long plane of trim but firm muscles. His red-rimmed steel gray eyes peered down at me over his narrow nose, though at five-nine, I wasn't that much shorter than him.

Still, his grim appearance was enough to make me shudder, like it was another rebuke on top of everything else that had gone wrong today.

"I guess I'll come back later," he said, turning on his heel.

"No, come in." I let out a sigh. Apparently, my thoughts had been enough to send out the "no vampires allowed" vibe that would have kept him from crossing my threshold.

"You sound so pleased to see me." Nonetheless, Draven stepped in. My intentions must have matched my words enough to let him know he was welcome.

Though I couldn't say it was ever a good sign for my vampire ex-boyfriend to show up on my doorstep these days.

Draven shuffled inside, looking around, his fists clenching tightly, as if he were stopping himself from bringing his hands out to inspect the cleanliness of my abode once more. We'd been there before.

Annoyed, I pushed a clay pot full of sunflower seeds I sometimes used for spells off a shelf, the dozens of dry seeds clattering to Draven's feet.

He jerked down before he could stop himself and started picking them up, counting them aloud as he added each one to the stack in his left palm.

Maybe I *was* wicked. Guilt and amusement warred within me as I watched him follow his compulsion through to the end. Once he had them all counted— thirty-seven—he dropped the pile back in the clay pot that now had a chip in it and glared up at me.

"Does my compulsion amuse you?" he asked dryly.

"Girl's gotta know how to distract a vampire from time to time," I said plainly instead of an apology. "Besides with a week-old coating of dust. NAELC," I said waving my arms lazily. Magic flowed from my fingers and dust soared into the sky from little knickknacks around the room. At least I wasn't entirely broken. I tried to avoid coughing as it all vanished, but apparently, I was not meant to look cool. "How can I help you?" I managed at last, the words escaping through a few bouts of hacking.

Maybe it'd been more than a week since I'd last cleaned.

Draven straightened and put the clay pot back on the shelf, shifting it a few extra times for good measure until he apparently decided it looked just right.

"What's biting you?" he asked, his focus still on the clay pot.

"Is that a joke?" I snapped.

He turned, his dark, red lips clamped together in a thin line. "It's clearly not me. Not in any sense of the word—unless you failed to tell me I annoyed you by trouncing you so thoroughly in Othello the other day."

Draven was a member of the Spooky Games Club, too. An original generation member, actually, considering he and Milton used to play in the first iteration long before I'd been born.

"Look, I've had a day," I said, leaning against the wall and crossing my arms.

"Clearly."

I scowled. "To what do I owe this visit?" I was in no mood to unload myself on him of all people.

"Sign-ups."

"Sign-ups?" What planet had this vampire descended from? "What are you talking about?"

"The Luna Lane Euchre Tournament. Cable sent me over here to make sure you're signing up."

There was so much surprising about that sentence, I didn't even know where to start.

My mind was so not present for this tournament. I'd almost forgotten about it entirely.

And Cable asking Draven to do something— and Draven doing it? Since when could Draven stand to converse with the attractive visiting professor, let alone plan a Games Club event with him?

"I don't even know how to play euchre," I said, voicing the third thing wrong with his sentence. And didn't Draven have a pub to run right now?

"That's what I thought." Draven nodded, examining me, then seemed to figure out what he was going to do. "Grab your shawl—everyone keeps telling me it's chilly out." A vampire wouldn't know.

"Because...?"

"Because practice is in session at First Taste."

The first thing that struck me as Draven held the door for me and I stepped inside First Taste, Luna Lane's only pub, was the laughter—louder even than the gentle rumbling sound effects of the fake thunderstorm that played over the pub's loud speakers.

There was an especially loud cackle that struck me with a wave of nostalgia.

"Ingrid," I said, remembering Cable had said she'd be arriving today.

"As feisty as ever," said Draven, closing the door behind us. We'd walked all this way in a brooding sort of silence, Broomie still sulking at home and Draven likely not about to turn into a bat and fly ahead of me, especially when I'd agreed to accompany him with all the enthusiasm of a grouch without her pile of garbage. Now the warm air inside the pub hit my windburned cheeks, and not even the mist the vampires had circulating from a smoke machine could dampen the feeling of relief that washed over my shoulders just then.

I wasn't alone. I might have been the only witch in town, but I didn't have to tackle everything on my own.

I too often needed reminders of that.

"Hey," I said as Draven went to slip past me. I found myself grabbing his cold, smooth-as-marble hand and squeezing it. "I'm sorry. For my attitude. For messing with you."

If blood could have circulated in his veins to color his cheeks, they might have darkened just then. His mouth curved into a flittering smile. "I think you've earned the chance to snap at me," he said. "What was it you called me when we broke up? 'A self-absorbed grump'?"

I winced and let his hand slip from mine. "Water over the bridge."

"Yes…" Draven's gaze flicked over me and he fingered one of the small chains protruding from the pant loops at his waist. "All in the past."

Despite his words, he looked about ready to pounce on me. I rubbed the side of my neck on instinct, as if to shield my jugular from his fangs.

"Is that Dahlia?" boomed a woman from across the pub.

All eyes seemed to turn on me and I rushed out

to meet Ingrid halfway to her table. She swept me up in a hug, the spritely, short and round woman practically lifting me off my feet. She stepped back and gave me a onceover, and I did the same. Her hair was pixie-short and all white now. Her brown eyes were as wide and round as I remembered and looked so much like her son's. Though wrinkles permeated her skin, she'd managed a soft, natural makeup to practically hide all the crinkles and creases. Her outfit—a pleated set of khakis and a plain white blouse—would have looked at home on some adventurer's show, though her clothes looked a bit faded from years of wear.

"You've grown up into such a wonderful young lady," she said, threading her arm through mine and directing me back to her table—or several tables pulled together.

"Want a drink?" asked Qarinah—gorgeous, shapely vampire, with long, silky black hair and pallid brown skin—from behind the bar.

Draven raised an eyebrow at me as he slipped behind her, as if to ask if I'd really go there.

He'd always made a sticking point of me being unable to handle my liquor when we'd dated—as if I even drank more than once or twice per month.

"Just seltzer, please," I said. Not because of Draven's unspoken objections, but because I needed a clear head.

Since Eithne had messed with me in the woods, it felt like an unseen clock hung overhead everywhere I went. Tick, tick, ticking down some kind of countdown to my doom.

I rubbed the stone scale on the back of my hand absentmindedly as I took a look at everyone gathered here.

Practically the whole, full-to-the-brim, no-one-had-any-excuses Spooky Games Club. Minus Faine, whom I imagined was busy not just with her family, but with prepping for Hungry Like a Pup's upcoming big Thanksgiving dinner.

There was Mayor Abdel, our mummy mayor, wrapped mostly in white cloth wrappings from head to toe, even under his suit, only a peek of his light brown complexion to be seen here and there. His light brown eyes and thin pink lips hinted at flesh that was hardly decayed beneath his enchanted wrappings—which had kept him alive for thousands of years.

Beside him was Chione, his great-great-great-too-many-greats-to-count granddaughter, whom he had invited to live with him in Luna Lane from Egypt some years back to help out at town hall. She was stunning, like a sculpture of an Egyptian queen, long, lanky limbs; sharp, angular features; smooth, pale brown skin; and tightly coiled black hair that she wore today pulled back into a ponytail at the top of her head.

Sheriff Roan Birch, the man most like a father to me, totally human and aged appropriately so, sat to her side, teasing his girlfriend, Qarinah, as she approached the table with my drink. He had a bit of a gut that hung over his sheriff's uniform, and his scalp shone from the large pink bald spot atop of it. The wrinkles at the corners of his eyes as he cackled were pronounced, but after handing me my drink, the stunning vampire Qarinah still looked as if she were blessed to have made him smile like that.

"Lia, don't just stand there. Sit down!" Roan gestured to the empty spot beside him I'd assumed was for Qarinah. Both she and Draven were in Games Club, though they didn't often show on the same nights. At least one of them liked to be at the bar during nighttime hours, though they had a small staff that ran the place during the day when they were asleep in their coffins.

Qarinah bustled back behind the counter to grab an empty mug from Jeremiah, Luna Lane's most productive farmer, who sat by himself at the counter, looking at the end of each day like something the cat had dragged in, disheveled and a tad dirty.

Then there was Goldie Mahajan, here without her husband, who only sometimes made it to club. She acknowledged me with a smile and a nod, but Ingrid had already made her way back to her end of the tables and they were chatting up a storm. Goldie wasn't in a sari for once—perhaps it was too cold. She had on a white cable-knit sweater decorated with festive turkeys. Her black-and-silver hair hung down over one shoulder.

Ginny the Luna Lane ghost wasn't here—she'd been one of the Games Club's most devoted members—but that wasn't surprising, considering all that had happened last month. She was either gone or still in hiding after she'd joined me for a quiet, solemn Halloween night.

Cable was notably absent, though there was an empty chair yet. But perhaps he'd stayed behind with Milton, who was part of the club since he usually hosted the meetings, but he wasn't always present enough to care to play for long.

There was someone I didn't recognize at all between Ingrid and Goldie.

An older woman, likely somewhere right between Ingrid's and Goldie's ages, so thin and fragile-looking, it looked as if her bones might have popped right through her mottled, wrinkled peach skin. Actually, she could have had decades on Ingrid, now that I examined her closer, though her face had retained some of its youthful luster and I could imagine her also being someone just newly retired. Her white hair reached her shoulders, her blue eyes almost too dark and speckled at both ends with a collection of moles or age spots. She also had on a knitted sweater, though it was a plain violet color somehow both classier and less fun than Goldie's own "ugly sweater" design.

"Oh, Dahlia, everyone else has been introduced." Ingrid shot back up again, far more spry than her years should have let her be. "This is Bette, my friend. She's traveling with me over the next few months."

Warily, I pulled my witch's hat down off my head, as if she wouldn't have noticed it already, my eyes flicking back and forth between Mayor Abdel and the out-of-towner.

"Oh, she knows." Ingrid fluffed a hand in my direction. "She's the one who told me about nymphs and golems in Europe."

I didn't think *I* had known that those were real. None had made their way to Luna Lane, anyway. It might have been a safe assumption that every myth had its roots in reality after living in a town with werewolves, vampires, and a ghost, but there were still some things that were fiction. Like chupacabras. I thought.

"Clay *and* stone golems," said Bette, nodding. "The latter of which is often mistaken for 'gargoyles.'" She picked up the stack of cards in front of her that someone had brought along and shuffled it, peering over at me, trying to get a feel for the resident witch, I could tell.

"You mean those monstrous beasts decorating French cathedrals?" Goldie asked.

"Well, not only France, but yes. My mother always told me they were spirits given form through enchantment."

"Who was your mother?" I wondered aloud. What kind of normie went around telling stories about the paranormal that an old, grown woman would take as fact long after her days of storybooks and fairy tales?

"No one anyone should find special, if that's what you mean." Bette smiled, cracking the chalky pink lipstick spread a little imperfectly on her lips. "But she knew witches. She was from the old country, and she grew up with witches in her village."

Ingrid let out a whistle, and I was still trying to think which "old country" she might have meant. The vampires often talked about Transylvania that way, but Bette's accent was more like a black-and-white movie star's than a European's.

"There are many places like Luna Lane throughout the globe," said Mayor Abdel cheerfully. "It's where we get many of our new residents." He winked at his granddaughter.

Faine's and Grady's extended families lived somewhere in northern Canada, in a werewolf village.

I supposed it wasn't too odd for there to be more normies who'd grown up amongst creatures most had only heard of in stories.

But what were the chances of her meeting Ingrid and coming here?

Bette stopped her card shuffling and looked around. "So two groups of four?"

I counted the table again. With me, that made seven.

"Thanks for waiting." Cable's deep, warm voice

echoed out from behind me as he approached from the direction of the restroom. "Dahlia! You came!"

Despite his words, he didn't seem to have doubted I would. As he slipped in the seat across from me, his dark eyes seemed soft, watching me with an inner glow.

Two seconds later, a bottle of cold beer rattled on the table between us. Draven hovered over my shoulder, and I looked up to find his thick lips in a scowl. "Can I get you anything else, Woodward?"

Cable, so easily jumpy about anything out of sorts, didn't even flinch as he picked up the bottle and took a sip. "No, thank you. Care to join us?"

"That would make us uneven," Bette said.

"I've got work to do," said Draven grimly. "But put me down for that tournament—I'll save my display of my talents for the moment when it actually matters."

The flesh on the back of his hand tightened as his fist formed, and he walked away. Ingrid, I realized, was watching the whole exchange with quite a bit of interest.

"Here, Dahlia, switch with me." Ingrid came around the table, leaving the seat next to her son wide open. "I'll play with Roan and the mayor. You can keep an eye on my son for me."

"*Mom.*" Cable fidgeted, pushing his glasses up his nose. But Ingrid was already shoving at my shoulders, brokering no argument.

"I don't even know how to play—" I started.

"Bette can teach you. She's a whiz at games." Ingrid winked.

When the seating had settled and Ingrid had produced another deck of cards to start a game up with the other end of the table, I found myself flush up against Cable, who scooted his chair closer as Bette began to deal out the cards.

"Usually, players are one a piece at each end of the table," said Bette. "Maybe we should pull the two tables apart again?"

The suggestion was like a splash of cold water over my face, as I realized Cable's thigh was touching mine and sending an exhilarating shiver right up my spine.

I wouldn't get many more chances to enjoy a fleeting moment like an unexpected touch.

"Good idea," said Ingrid, and then the moment was gone.

Roan and Cable got up to help shift the tables apart, and soon I had a whole side of it to myself.

Not used to meeting new people, I felt awkward across from Bette, still depressed over the day's events. I wanted to tell someone everything—but which of my friends, and what good would it do?

I needed to figure out what had gone wrong when I'd tried to summon my mother. I needed to focus on stopping Eithne from doing any more damage—to me or to anyone else in Luna Lane.

But my time with Cable was growing short, and he seemed so enthused about this tournament.

Besides, what other than the upcoming Thanksgiving dinner would be the most likely to attract a troublemaker like Eithne's attention?

The Euchre Tournament.

The past two months, her shadow had lingered over not one, but two Spooky Games Club events.

Summon my mother. Stop Eithne. Break my curse.

The ball of anxiety in my stomach wasn't going to help me figure out anything.

"Have you played euchre before, Goldie?" Bette asked, dealing out the cards in a strange fashion. She sent multiple cards to each player, and the number wasn't always the same.

At the next table over, Ingrid was regaling her audience with some tale about chartering a plane and crossing the Mediterranean.

"Oh, yes," said Goldie. "Though it's been years. The boys grew up and moved out—and they weren't keen to play games with their parents some years before that."

So it was just me who was the amateur? Why was I going to bother participating in this tournament? I could be just as effective watching from the sidelines, looking for signs of anything amiss.

Mom and I had played a card game or two when Roan had stopped by. But it looked like this was a four-player game. "I know nothing about it."

"I could use a refresher," said Cable, picking up the cards she'd dealt him.

I sent him a grateful look.

Bette let out a little "hmm" noise as she looked from Cable to me and back again. Feeling my face flush, I picked up my own cards and focused pointedly at them.

"You play euchre in two teams of two," said Bette. "So how should we split this up? An experienced member with a newcomer, perhaps?" She looked pointedly at me, then offered Goldie a dazzling smile. "You up for pairing with Ingrid's handsome boy?"

Goldie straightened in her seat. "Yes, of course. We'll do our best." She giggled as she stared over her cards at Cable.

"That leaves you and me," Bette said to me.

Yes. Wonderful. I didn't know why that bothered me so, but I had to suppress a shiver as I nodded at her, staring very hard at my queen of hearts.

"We'll make a great team." Bette's smile was just too sweet. "There are twenty-four cards in play"— she gestured toward the playing card box, which wasn't empty, I realized—"aces through nines of each suit. Some people play with the joker, but I feel simple is best for those still lacking experience."

The way she spoke was just so condescending. I had to remind myself this was a tournament—open to the public—but I just had to bite back the thought that she was making the Spooky Games Club less fun than it ought to have been if we'd just stuck to playing among friends.

Then again, if we managed to get through this

without any dead bodies, I'd have to acknowledge the quality of Games Club's activities was improving.

"What's the objective again?" Cable scratched the back of his head, his attention drawn to the cards in his hand as he rearranged them.

"Take more tricks than the other team," said Goldie, studying her card as well.

"Tricks?" I asked when no one else did.

"The player with the highest trump card wins the trick," said Bette, her white eyebrow arched as she gazed at her own cards.

"Ace is high in this one?" Cable offered.

Goldie nodded. "And nine is the lowest." She was all business now. She clearly remembered this game better than she'd insisted.

"But any card of the trump suit of the round is still higher in value than any other card," said Bette.

Goldie and Cable nodded, the former pursing her lips. They were already formulating strategies in their heads while I was just trying to keep up.

"*But* the jack of the trump suit is actually worth the most—it's called the right bower," Bette added.

"Oh, oh, and the jack of the suit of the same color is the left bower, right?" added Goldie helpfully. "It's coming back to me."

I slapped a hand to my forehead. "Wait, so you're saying... If the trump suit is hearts, the jack of hearts, not the ace of hearts, is the highest-ranking card. And the jack of *diamonds* is the second highest—despite everything else you just said?"

"Yes," said Bette simply.

"Okay…" I let out a sigh and shuffled my cards together by suit, for lack of something else to do. "Who decides the trump suit?"

"The kitty," Cable explained. So even he knew that much. He nodded toward the middle of the table, where four other cards were still face down. "That's the kitty. The top card is flipped over, and that determines the trump suit for the round."

"I think we're losing her." Bette's eyes sparkled mischievously as she stared at me over her cards. "Don't worry about what the dealer does. We'll have someone deal for you when it's your turn."

I bristled and clutched my cards tighter in my clammy hands. "What else do I need to know?" If everyone else could keep up, so would I.

"When it's your turn, you can decide to play or pass," said Goldie. "If we all pass, the whole kitty will be set aside."

"Okay…" I'd follow their lead, I supposed. "So if we all pass, what's the trump suit?"

"Then the next player can call a different trump suit," said Bette smugly. "But I'd only recommend that if you have three or more cards of the same color in hand. Perhaps we should play a round where we can see all of your cards and give you advice."

Instinctively, I brought my hand closer to my

chest, as if I didn't want my own teammate to pry them from me.

"It's really such a simple game," said Bette, fluffing at her white curls. "Nothing like poker or rummy."

My jaw clenched as I took another look at my cards. "What if I don't have a card from the trump suit?"

"Then you can play any other card," said Goldie. "Aim for your highest value—because each trick is over fast, and the player with the highest value card played wins."

"If you can't play the trump suit, your chances of winning are nil. But you should still play your best. The same color suit as the trump suit is higher value than the opposite color," said Bette smoothly.

That I could follow. "So if the trump suit is hearts, then the nine of diamonds is worth more than the ace of spades or clubs?"

"Yes, but not as much as any heart card." Goldie looked at me like a proud teacher.

"There are five tricks per hand, and the team with the most wins declares victory," said Bette, not brooking any nonsense like acknowledging I'd gotten one thing right.

"So for this tournament, there're going to be two winners?" I asked.

"If we decide on teams from the start, I imagine so," Bette replied. "Though a player can call a lone."

"A loan?" I asked. "Borrowing cards?"

Bette's laughter was shrill. "No, dear. A *lone*. Like a lone hand. They play alone for all five tricks in a hand because they think they have enough of the highest-value cards to claim victory."

"I…" My mouth gaped open. I was never going to remember all of this.

"But the lone round still counts for the team's win. Is that an issue for you?" Bette asked. "Playing in teams?"

"Of course not." My eyes flitted tellingly to Cable beside me. There was a wrinkle in his brow as he studied his cards. It gave him a rather attractive, studious look, and I wondered if any of his students had crushes on him.

The errant thought made half the rules of euchre fly out of my head. If only we'd stuck to sitting opposite one another—not just because we could have teamed up, but because he wouldn't have been so distractingly close.

Bette's gaze narrowed on me. "There are a few more rules, like keeping track of points each hand to determine who wins a match and when the game is over, but you just leave that to the experienced hands." Her grin practically dazzled, and I noticed how straight and white her teeth were. They had to be fakes to be that great at her age—though they were missing that artificial sheen.

"Wait, but why is it called euchre?" I asked. "What's a euchre?"

"I don't think *a euchre* is a thing outside of this game." Now even Goldie was giggling at me.

"Euchre is what happens when someone gets cocky and falls flat on their face. If a team that names the trump winds up losing the trick, that's said to be euchre for the opposing team." Bette played with a golden chain around her neck. It dipped down beneath her sweater, keeping whatever charm it might have carried out of view. "Kind of like the opposing team cheated you out of your rightful win. Isn't that marvelous? I do love a difficult win like that."

Bette was sizing me up and down now. I felt suddenly grateful to be on her team because I was about to unintentionally throw the game and I could drag her down with me. Unless she played *alone*.

"We'll be sure to point out any faux pas as you play," said Bette. "Ready?" She'd talked so quickly, I hardly felt ready at all, but I was the only one not to nod my assent. Bette turned over the top of the kitty to reveal the king of clubs. "Okay, then. Let's start. It sounds like the other table has quite a lead on us already."

Next table over, Chione let out a little sequel of delight. She must have won a trick.

"So where do you hail from, Bette?" asked Goldie as she took the first turn, naming clubs the trump suit and playing the ace.

"Well, Ingrid and I met up at a museum in

Salem," said Bette. It was my turn. What card did I play? I had a club... A nine, of course. How helpful.

"Massachusetts?" Cable asked. He played the queen of clubs. So he'd never met his mom's friend, either?

Bette nodded. "We're both avid travelers. I've hardly ever spent time at home the past decade. It's my bucket list to see as many sites of... supernatural interest as possible."

"Like Luna Lane?" I offered dryly.

"Exactly like Luna Lane. Well, someone like me wouldn't have known about Luna Lane, so it hadn't made the cut originally. But you know. Salem, Roswell... I've already done a tour of Europe and Asia." She played the jack of clubs and that was it. Our team had won the trick. That went fast. A euchre win already. She placed a card from her hand onto the table. Nine of hearts.

"How remarkable! Did you swing by India?" Goldie asked. She played a card. It wasn't a heart. She frowned after she put it down, then stared at her hand again, then rubbed her forehead.

"Of course." Bette's smile was warm, though her makeup caked and cracked whenever her face flexed. "And might I say, you do remind me so of an apsara I met there."

It took Goldie a moment to even respond. "Excuse me," she said, blinking. "I had a bit of a headache there." But she blushed and laughed when she seemed to realize what Bette had said, suddenly looking much brighter, as if the headache had already passed. "Thank you. Perhaps it was my sister from another mister." She'd often joked about being related to an apsara.

"You've met an apsara?" I asked. "In the flesh?" I realized it was my turn, so I threw out my queen of hearts. Then I stiffened when I realized I was holding the jack of diamonds, too. That was worth more now, wasn't it? Left man bowing or something...

"Yes," said Bette. She pinched her lips, almost as if she knew I'd made a mistake. "As beautiful as you'd expect a goddess to be. Don't you believe in them? You seemed surprised when Ingrid mentioned nymphs and golems before."

So my worldly knowledge was a little lacking. I had a good excuse. "I'm just surprised anyone of the paranormal persuasion would reveal themselves so readily, that's all."

Bette's mouth was stern, her eyebrow arched as she focused on her cards, as if holding back a biting comment.

"Mom was less interested in supernatural things when I was growing up—we visited normal human historical monuments and unexplored parts of countries. Nothing special." Cable seemed to be examining his cards, too, coming up with some kind of strategy despite keeping up with the conversation. He played the ace of hearts.

Nothing special? "Must be from growing up

surrounded by all that," I offered. "It'd just seem normal to you. I'd find *any* of it fascinating. More fascinating than the supernatural I see every day."

"You don't seem a very worldly witch, forgive me saying," snapped Bette, as if *my* remark had offended *her* somehow.

The table went quiet, the laughter echoing out from Ingrid's happier bout of euchre enough to make me envious of those of us who were enjoying themselves at this game.

"Dahlia can't leave town," said Goldie quietly for me.

"Oh?" Bette looked me over, her gaze focusing very hard on my arm. "I would have thought you would have, to see more of your kind. There are no other witches or gargoyles like you here, or so Ingrid tells me."

The stone scales on my arm tingled as the hair on my other arm stood up straight.

Had she just called me a… gargoyle?

Chapter Five

"*No other—*" My mouth gaped open and I put my cards down on the table, rubbing my arm. "I'm a witch. Just a witch."

"Forgive me," said Bette, following suit and laying her own cards face-down. "The stone pattern all over your arm—I was sure it meant you were part gargoyle."

Now she had me doubting what I knew to be true. I stared at my arm. "I've never even *met* a gargoyle."

"Dahlia was cursed," said Goldie, and I winced, trying to send her silent vibes not to spill my life story to this woman.

I'd only known Bette a few minutes and I already didn't like her. She knew more than enough about me, about this town—but I supposed Luna

Lane wasn't anything impressive to a world-weary supernatural-seeking traveler like her.

Bette wouldn't stop staring at my arm. "By a gargoyle?"

"No, not by a gargoyle!" This time, I pushed my chair back. This day just was determined to keep me grouchy. "How could I have been cursed by a gargoyle if I've never even met one?"

Now the whole bar was looking at me—though thankfully, it was mostly just my friends.

"I didn't realize gargoyles were known for curses," offered Cable, tapping the table with his knuckle, as if to ward off a jinx. "I just thought they were like... Protectors. Of cathedrals and other gothic things."

"Protectors they may be," said Bette smoothly, picking up her cards once more. She finally took her turn, laying down the jack of hearts. Seriously? Did she have all the jacks in that hand and if so, why wasn't she calling a lone hand? Why make me struggle my way through this game I could barely keep track of? "If the witch who brought them to life wants them to be. But golems—stone or otherwise—can be adversaries, too." Her eyes narrowed on me. "If their creators so desire them to be."

"I'll be sure to keep that in mind." I picked up my cards, my knee bobbing irritably as I sat back too far from the table. "If one should ever flap its stony wings over to Luna Lane."

Bette *tsked* as she laid down a ten of spades and

called the next trump suit. "Do you know a witch's weakness?"

"Condescending them to death?" I offered dryly.

Bette pinched her lips. "Merely making conversation."

Conversation? But was she telling me *she* knew a witch's weakness or was she hoping I'd tell her it so she could get one over on me?

I couldn't dignify either possibility with a comment.

Cable kept tapping the table with a fidgety finger. "So, Goldie, how are Zashil and Javier doing?" They were Goldie's son and son-in-law.

Goldie's gaze flicked in Bette's direction as she played her king of spades. *Now* she seemed wary about the newcomer knowing too much. "They love it in Atlanta already," she said hesitatingly. "Zashil was never meant for small town living, I know that now. Perhaps it was all for the best. Zashil is talking about going back to school to get his master's in business now."

His dream of owning and operating an escape room had been tainted, I knew that—but still, it had been sad to see him go. He'd flit right back into life here in Luna Lane and then had flit right back out. There was a whole world of opportunities out there, I knew that, but that wasn't true for everyone.

Certainly not for me. I added a nine of spades to the pile. Between the hand I'd been dealt and my own mistakes, I was just coasting along with Bette's wins at the moment.

Cable put down the ace of spades card and smiled. "I think that means I win the trick?"

Bette's head bobbed as she examined the table thoroughly, as if there were some magic sprites hidden beneath the playing cards or something. "So it seems. You remember more about this game than you thought."

"Muscle memory." Cable flexed his arm, and my eyes widened to see the solid, thick biceps I'd only guessed were there pop distinctly.

Goldie laughed as her eyebrows wriggled at me.

"I think I get the gist of it," I said, laying my cards face-up on the table. "Maybe I should get going."

"But we haven't even finished the hand." Goldie *tsked* me.

Bette's stern eyes turned on my exposed cards. "The 'hang of it,' huh? Where was that jack of diamonds two tricks ago?"

She'd caught me. So I wasn't winning any tournament. I'd live down the shame.

She sighed. "Well, with her cards out in the open like that, I guess the match is over. Prematurely. Let's try this again." She started collecting everyone's cards, and I went to stand before she dealt another hand.

"When is the tournament again?" I asked, turning to Cable. He was the organizer, after all.

"Tomorrow night," he said.

"Arjun and I are offering up a ham *and* a turkey for the winners," said Goldie excitedly. She and her husband ran Vogel's, the one general store in town. "I know Faine is going to make a delicious Thanksgiving dinner, but you can always cook the prizes another time."

"Faine might take the prize home herself," said Cable with a wink. "She seems quite excited about this whole tournament idea."

As if to punctuate the feeling that everyone but me was feeling enthused about it, the cries of "Whoa!" from the table over led me to believe someone had turned some unexpected trick.

"What time?" I asked. "And where?"

"Here. Seven o'clock." Cable gestured around him. "Both Draven and Qarinah want to participate, so we thought it best to just hold it here so one or the other can keep serving while the tournament is in play."

"You take these," said Bette. She'd apparently gathered all of our cards into a pile and slipped them into the box decorated in green and red, then she slid the box toward me across the table. "Maybe practice before tomorrow."

My eyelid twitched as I stared the tiny old lady down. I'd never met someone who'd aggravated me so quickly—who'd made me feel it was so personal, too.

"I think I have a deck at home." I shoved the

cards back. "You can keep playing. Ask Qarinah or Draven to jump in or something."

Bette slid them back toward me. "You can never have too many decks of playing cards. Entertaining, traveling—they're good to have on hand. Fills the moments of boredom." She had a hard, perceptible jawline. "Oh, but you can't travel, can you?"

I gripped the edge of the table, just stopping myself from flipping it over at her, then flicked the card box back to her, the clink of my stone scale on the back of my hand against the cardboard hard to ignore. "I have no one to practice with before tomorrow."

Bette slid the box back. "Then maybe enjoy some solitaire. It's good for the brain. Keeps it sharp." She tapped the side of her temple, her pale eyes glinting.

Before I could shove them back, Goldie stood and snatched the cards off the table and waited for me to hold out my hand. Reluctantly, I held out my palm and she dropped the box into it. "Bring it to Vogel's tomorrow and we'll play. You, me, Arjun —Broomie?"

"Broomie?" asked Bette sharply.

"I'm busy tomorrow," I said simply, turning on my heel. "But thank you." Rather than argue about it any longer, I popped open the pouch on the golden belt on my waist and slid the box inside.

With a start, my fingers warmed as the box slid past them and inside the pouch. Like the box had moved at such high friction, it could have burned me. I touched them again, but the sensation had faded, the warmth more like that of an object that had just been clutched in a sweaty palm.

The box felt heavy in my pouch at my hip. I turned to Bette, but she was already making her way over to the other table, leaning over Ingrid and whispering to her, the two laughing as Ingrid rearranged her cards in her hand. Goldie joined them, staring over Roan's shoulder at the table.

"How well do you know Bette?" I asked Cable quietly.

Cable paused to examine me. "I just met her tonight. But Mom often picks up a new friend for a leg or two of her never-ending journey. She's affable like that. Why do you ask?"

"You don't find it odd she brought a friend who knows about the paranormal?"

"I would hope she wouldn't bring a friend who didn't, considering how protective some of Luna Lane's residents are about your 'secret.'" He playfully nudged me, his arm against my shoulder.

I felt my prickly defenses melting at that.

"It's just... Never mind." The laughter ringing out from the other table painted a rosy sheen over any of my doubts. "I've had a long, long day."

Sighing, I turned on my heel to find Draven staring daggers at me—or at the back of Cable's head—from behind the bar.

"Do you want to talk about it?" Cable asked.

At just that moment, Ingrid cried out triumphantly, hitting Chione's hand for a high five across the table. As Ingrid gathered the cards, she shifted in her seat to look over her shoulder at us. "Cable, Dahlia, come over here! We can mix up the teams!"

"Can I get a practice round in?" asked Qarinah, shuffling past her sullen bar co-owner and dropping a rag in a bin behind the counter. "Someone needs to teach me how to play before tomorrow."

Roan's eyes lit up as she made her way toward the table.

Ingrid cocked her head. "But then we'll have nine."

"You play," I said to Qarinah. "I'm going home anyway."

Cable leaned closer, his eyebrows drawing together. "Did anything happen?"

I thought about telling him. Would worry about Eithne keep Cable from leaving for his short trip? It couldn't keep him here forever. Besides, did I want that? To force him to be as stuck as me?

"Nothing. Nothing new."

I could tell Faine—but she was busier this week than ever. I didn't want to add to her burdens.

Roan might want to know… But just then, he looked so happy as Qarinah took Ingrid's seat kitty-corner from him.

And Draven… Draven was wiping a glass so hard right now, his expression so sharp, I thought the glass might shatter in his hand. I'd annoyed him enough for one day.

Tomorrow. I'd figure out what to do tomorrow.

"I'll see you tomorrow," I said, making my way to the door.

"Seven o'clock!" Cable said. "For the tournament."

Right. For the tournament.

Weariness must have pervaded my bones because Mom's old cuckoo clock struck ten A.M. by the time I woke up.

I stretched beneath my floral comforter, wriggling my toes.

Broomie leaped out of nowhere at the foot of my bed to launch her bristly brush all over my moving feet, "munching" on them like she would a cornhusk.

Crying out at first, I started laughing, extending my hands toward her.

She flew up and curled up in my arms. "Am I forgiven?" I asked.

As if to answer, she wriggled her brush even more against my chest.

"I'm sorry I snapped at you," I said. "I wasn't thinking straight."

Today, with a good night's sleep and a clearer mind, I would be.

"Let's go get some ingredients for my power-boosting brews," I said.

This time, I would summon Mom for sure. If last time had been the final time she could venture back here, surely, she would have known. Surely, she would have told me.

Though the last line she'd uttered *had* been cut short.

Broomie made a rustling, almost sad sound and pointed her head at the cuckoo clock.

I knew I shouldn't, but… "We'll be back in time to perform a deed." We had to be. Gathering ingredients would take an hour at most, and then Mom wouldn't be able to stay long.

I'd find out more from her, then make my way to someone in need of my help, someone who could listen to all my worries and help me keep an eye out tonight.

Sheriff Roan would be working by the time I went to tell him, so he couldn't blame me for putting a damper on his day.

Yes. That was the plan.

I quickly got dressed, flinging open my wardrobe and selecting a plain purple dress with long sleeves. My fingers briefly caressed the black-and-purple ballgown Spindra had made for me and Ginny had presented to me. Strangely, the first thing that popped in my mind was the fact that no one but Ginny had seen me in it. If I'd worn it and invited Cable to

my Halloween celebration, would he have…
Would we have…?

I dismissed those thoughts. The idea of parting from Cable for just a few weeks was messing with my head. I had to look at it as practice for when he left for good in a few short months.

I got dressed, waving my hands at myself and muttering, "NAELC." I really wasn't fond of bathing the way the normies did. All that water dried out my skin.

The enchantment took, but it was like my magic needed a moment to warm up, the enchantment more draining than it ought to have been.

Broomie tilted her brush as if to cock her head, observing my frown.

She was still moving. So if there was any para-paranormal nearby, it was weak—distant or small in amount, or both.

But it couldn't be too far or I wouldn't have felt its effects at all.

With a start, I ran for my golden belt, which I'd hung with my hat on the rack by the front door.

Broomie lingered behind me in the hallway, watching me from a safe distance as I fumbled open the pouch.

Her wariness proved it, didn't it?

I pulled the deck of cards out, expecting it to burn—or at least feel warm—in my hand.

But it didn't.

Then again, I'd played with these cards last

night and hadn't felt anything off with them. Not until I'd slipped them into my pouch.

I opened the deck and shuffled the cards in my hand, feeling nothing resembling the warm sensation I'd felt last night. Tossing the cards down on the table near the door, I focused on the box the cards had come in.

Still, nothing.

Had I just imagined the warm sensation from the cards? Many enchantments left a briefly lived residue from all that energy that might be construed as warmth if an enchanted object were held in one's hands, but... If Bette were a witch, I would have noticed her casting the enchantment. Unless she were as powerful as Eithne and didn't need to say a word to work magic.

But still. I was sure I'd have noticed *something*.

Was it possible my sluggish enchantment was just the result of stress and being tired?

I swapped the box for the pile of cards in my hand once more, determined to fish through the cards more slowly, get a feel for what each individual might have been hiding.

There was a knock on the door behind me and I jumped, the cards fluttering out of my hand and scattering everywhere.

If it was Draven at the door, I could count on him to pick them up for me, though I thought if I remembered right, the compulsion might have been related only to very small, grain- or seed-like objects.

I opened the door. Cable stood on the other side of it, his breath just slightly visible in the crisp November air.

"Cable!" Despite temporarily living next door and helping me clean up my garden last month from time to time, the visiting professor had never really shown up at my doorstep. At least not alone.

"May I come in?" he asked, reminding me sharply in that moment of Draven.

But no. The smile on Cable's face was restrained, but he couldn't stop it from lighting up his dark eyes.

I couldn't even imagine the man ever being sullen.

"Of course." I stepped aside.

Cable's mouth downturned when he noticed the game of Fifty-Two Pickup I'd unintentionally started. "Am I interrupting... something?"

It was chilly in here. I laughed as I shut the door behind him, waving my arms at the fireplace beyond my runes circle. "ERIF." It worked. More proof that I was just imagining the sluggishness, that there was nothing in the cards that would hurt me. The logs collected there crackled to life, the cast-iron cauldron hung above it empty, but in no danger just from being lit without a concoction inside. I cleaned it thoroughly whenever used. "I was just about to go out to gather some ingredients in the woods, but I have a minute."

Cable, his wool coat still on, bent down to start picking up the cards for me.

"Oh, I—" I could have enchanted them all together with a wave of my hand, but I appreciated the gesture. I crouched down beside him to start picking up the cards the human way. They really had spread far and wide across the room. I spotted one under the couch and made my way over there, shuffling on my knees.

Just as I stretched my hand under there, Cable let out a harried, small scream behind me.

I knew that scream and what kind of mischief usually accompanied it.

"Broomhilde," I said sharply, spinning around.

Her bristles shook as she popped out from beneath the lapel of Cable's coat. She must have found him on his hands and knees and used his distraction to fly right up and through his coat to surprise him.

Cable was jumping, spinning around in circles, as if a snake were in there and not my companion broomstick. The cards he'd managed to collect fluttered back to the floor, scattering widely once more.

"Just stay still!" I said to Cable, standing up and tossing what cards I had on the couch. "*Broomhilde*, you know better than to scare him like that. Come out here right now."

Broomie did try to squirm up and out, but her

bristles brushed against Cable's cheek, knocking his glasses askew. She tugged and he flailed more, his coat stretching at odd angles, but Broomie found no escape route. Now *she* was panicking, her movements too quick, too harried, as Cable tried in vain to straighten his glasses, his feet stumbling as he toppled over the little table by the door, then the hat rack, my hat scurrying outward and slipping to my feet.

"Both of you, calm down!" I snatched my hat and slapped it on my head, extending my arms out toward them. "SEHTOLC S'ELBAC EVOMER!"

I one hundred percent should have known better.

I absolutely should have said, "TAOC" instead of "SEHTOLC." It was a Freudian slip of the worst proportions, but in the panic of the moment, of the two of them acting as if they'd been irrevocably melded at the hip instead of simply tangled up, that was the enchantment that escaped my lips.

Chapter Six

*a*t least Broomie was able to untangle herself as soon as his coat unbuttoned and plunged to the floor.

After that, though, our problems only grew. First one of Cable's feet and then the other lifted as his shoes and even socks flew off. And then came the button-down pale blue dress shirt and the fly at the khakis and instead of *doing something* helpful, I let out a pitiful yelp, covered my eyes, and spun on my heel.

But not before, I'm sorry to say, his white undershirt flew off and I got a nice, good look at those muscles dotting his torso and upper arms.

He really *did* have no business looking so finely sculpted with his nose in a book most of the time.

Despite myself, I giggled, loosening the last bit of tension that had been tearing at my body down to its very core. Clutching the back of the couch, I bowled over. "I'm sorry," I said, though there was far too little weight behind the apology, considering I was laughing so much. "I'm so, so, so sorry."

Behind me, Cable let out a little grunt and there was a zipping noise. "Well… I might have just stopped at the coat if I were you, but thank you. I guess." There was one clunk and then the other, and I imagined he was getting his shoes back on after zipping up his pants.

Broomie's brush shook beside me and she kept turning her broom to peer back at Cable, then letting out one of her bristling giggles again. "Stop that," I said, batting her—not too hard, of course. "You need to say you're sorry. And don't do such a thing again! Cable has been nothing but nice to you."

Her brush turned again, and for just a moment, I envied her innocence in that she got to keep looking at him with impunity despite causing the whole mess. Well, a good portion of the mess.

Broomie floated back toward him, but I couldn't in good conscience do more than clutch the back of the couch harder and refuse to look.

"All right, you're sorry." Cable spoke over the sound of loud, bristly friction of bristles on skin. "All right, all right." This time, he chuckled. "Oh, you can look now, Dahlia."

Wincing, I turned on my heel.

Broomie was rubbing against Cable repeatedly,

from his legs all the way up to his stubbly cheek, though she was jostling the glasses again. Cable's shirt still hung open unbuttoned, his undershirt clinging so tightly to his mess of muscles like melted butter.

"I'm sorry," I said again, shaking out my arms before clasping my hands together. This time, I managed to apologize without the laughter.

Cable's cheeks flushed as he stared at me, patting Broomie's shaft. "At least you didn't transform any part of me this time."

"Everything was right where it was supposed to be?" I teased, the words out of my mouth before I could stop them.

He looked downward in a panic. "Should I have inspected everything closer?"

That made me crack up once more.

"You're fine. You should be. My enchantment worked only on your clothes—though I should have specified 'coat.'"

"Hmm. Easy enough mistake—when you have to take the time to speak a word backward." Cable's head tilted as he inspected me suspiciously.

I threw up my hands in surrender. "I know how it seems. Believe me or not, I really didn't think it through."

"I believe you," he said, his face flushing nevertheless. Broomhilde wandered over to the kitchen as Cable finished buttoning up his shirt. My stomach rumbled and reminded me that I far too often forewent meals when my mind was preoccupied.

I was only trying to break my curse and prevent Eithne from causing any more destruction in my town, after all.

"Can I get you anything?" I asked. "Coffee?" I opened a cupboard, pretty bare. "Um... Crackers or peas?"

Cable chuckled. "I swung by to see how you were doing—but maybe we should get a bite?"

"How I was doing?" I spun on my heel. Broomie nudged her empty food bowl toward me, as if to remind me about her cornhusks. She could live without them but preferred not to when corn was in season, especially.

"You seemed... out of sorts last night."

I bit my lip. I needed to tell someone anyway. "Don't you have planning to do? For the tournament tonight?"

Cable fluffed a hand in the air. "There wasn't much to it. We booked the venue, came up with the prize—Mom said she'll get Bette and Milton to help with a little advertising today. It's not like it's a professional-level event."

"It *is* the Spooky Games Club's first big event, though," I pointed out.

"Want to help with the decorations?"

I glanced at my runes circle behind Cable, at the scattered cards all over the place. "I would, but I really have something I need to get done today."

"Ingredients for potions?"

"Yeah."

"But have you done your good deed yet?"

I let out a sigh. There were only so many hours in the day, and too often, I had to dwell on how to squeeze a good deed into them.

"Eithne is back," I said simply, as if that would explain everything.

Perhaps it did. A sense of dread washed over Cable's face. "You saw her?"

"I did. Yesterday. In the woods."

"Why didn't you say anything yesterday?" Cable moved across the room to the kitchen, his eyebrows drawing together as he neared.

"I didn't want... Everyone was so happy and busy, and I didn't want to bother them. Not before I'd had a chance to uncover more answers."

Cable's hand clutched my arm, his warmth sending a shiver down my spine. "Dahlia, you should know by now not to take everything on by yourself. Busy? Busy with what?"

"The tournament, your trip..."

"And neither is as important as keeping you safe." Cable looked down at his hand and seemed to only just then realize he was clutching me. He let his grip fall.

"And keeping *the town* safe," I said, reprimanding myself. "Cable, to tell the truth, I was a little worried about this tournament once Eithne showed her face—"

"Did she say anything about it?"

"No. We didn't talk about it at all. But you know how she seems to have had a hand in every memorable event over the past two months."

"Oh, I don't know about that." The corners of Cable's lips twitched. "I have a lot of fond memories no evil witch has tarnished of my time in Luna Lane."

I was glad *he* at least could take the attempted and successful murders in stride. As if there were something more hopeful and happy for him to associate his time here with.

Whatever it was must have been a very potent happy sensation indeed.

"Do you think we should cancel?" Cable frowned.

"The tournament?" I chewed the inside of my cheek. "Maybe? I don't know. But everyone should be on alert." I scoffed. "You're right. I don't know what I was thinking. You need to spread the word."

"*I* need to?"

I opened the box of crackers and started scarfing down as many as I could. "I need to figure out what, exactly, she's up to. And for that, I need ingredients for a power boost."

Cable looked at me skeptically, watching me stuff crackers in my mouth like a parrot. "Dahlia, you have to eat."

"I *am* eating," I mumbled between bites. "But that reminds me, when you swing by Vogel's to warn the Mahajans, can you have Goldie send some more cornhusks my way?"

Broomie zipped up high into the air and nodded her brush excitedly.

"You have a good deed to complete yet—"

"I'll do it before nightfall. I promise."

Cable sighed and took off his glasses, inspecting the lenses for dirt—or maybe scratches, considering the broom that had been all up in his face. "I'll be back to check on you."

"Sure, sure." I stuffed the last of the sleeve of crackers into my mouth and chewed rapidly. "I'll be done in a couple of hours—plenty of time before the tournament."

My trip with Broomie to the woods actually had gone smoothly. We'd gotten everything we'd needed for several vials' worth of a couple of simple power-boosting concoctions, and we'd come home to a bucket of cornhusks on the porch for Broomie.

Now, she was munching on her treat in the kitchen while I was mixing my second vial of the rose-colored potion, some of the more foul pine-needle-based power boosters already brewed. The fire I'd relit upon returning home was crackling, the sun just barely streaming in through the kitchen window. It was overcast, but daylight was already pretty sparse this time of year.

"One more pinch of salt," I said, my eyes roving over the open page in Mom's potions book. I knew these two power-boosting potions by heart—one, it claimed for strength of magic, the other for strength of purpose—but I was too wary of too many things having gone wrong in my life to risk getting anything wrong in the mixture. I had no other witch to rely on for guidance, of course. It was all my experience and this book, my mother's teachings forming the backbone—but they'd proven, I'd discovered in the years since her passing, just to be the surface of that which a witch was capable.

My feet shuffled across the pile of the playing cards still scattered about on the floor, forgotten in my haste to get Cable out the door to warn everyone and be on my way. I reached the kitchen and the salt shaker, groaning under my breath to find it running so low. Vogel's was across the street, yet I too often forgot to do my regular shopping. I was a poor cook and too often focused on things besides the basics I needed to do, like eating.

And my good deed.

As if to remind me of that, my mom's cuckoo clock went off down the hall. Three o'clock already. But I had a couple of hours before sundown.

"Just finish this, and you'll have some extras on hand." As I walked back toward the potion-brewing table beside my rune circle, my feet sent a pile of cards flying, one of which kicked up into the air and soared straight over my rune circle and into my lit fire.

The explosion that followed registered for all of two seconds before I was sent flying and blacked out.

Chapter Seven

*B*ristles against my face. Broomie's brush chomping on my toes.

I kicked at her gently, to beg her to let me sleep a moment more.

But she was insistent, her bristles coming down like teeth until I let out a scream and jumped up.

I was on the ground in the living room, up against my couch. My neck had been bent at a painful angle.

I went to soothe my aching muscles and let out another howl as the movement of my left arm seared with pain more intense than in any other part of me.

I gazed down at my wrist to find a stone scale that took up the entire inner forearm, from my wrist down to my elbow—a scale that had definitely not been there before. The edges were rimmed in pink, and it itched something fierce.

Most alarmingly, turning my hand, bending my elbow, proved a strain—possible but difficult, as if the heaviness in my limb was working against me.

"What… What happened? What time is it?" I blinked furiously, and as if in answer, Mom's cuckoo clock struck seven.

Seven.

But where was Cable? Why hadn't he come back to check on me?

Broomie shook her bristles hard and stretched out as far as she could, pointing in the direction of the fireplace. The fire was out, the wood far too charred and still smoking when it should have been extinguished by now. Around it, everything was shifted, broken, blackened. Even the impenetrable cauldron was cracked down the middle, like it had absorbed the brunt of the impact. All of my vials of potions were shattered, the contents oozing out. Some of it bubbled as two strong concoctions mixed when they weren't supposed to.

There were black streaks across my rune circle, leaving gaps in the design.

"No, no, no, no." I crawled forward on sore knees and shins, gesturing vaguely at my whole body and murmuring, "LAEH," but barely registering it.

Everywhere except my fresh scale, the pain retreated.

But not the feeling of dread that struck deep within my heart.

My fingers traced over the gaps in the rune

circle, and I stared at the bubbling mess everywhere around me. "YDIT," I said through a hiccupping sob. "NAELC."

The room rearranged itself, tidying up of all the debris, the soot and ash fading.

"XIF," I said to the room. The vials melded together, empty, but no longer broken. The nearby shelving repaired itself. The cauldron forged into one piece.

But the circle remained scuffed. The ash marks scrubbed away, but the gaps in the circle remained as clear as day.

"RIAPER!" I held both hands over the circle. "ELCRIC ENUR RIAPER!" But nothing happened.

I started sobbing and sunk down.

Without a working rune circle, there was so much magic I couldn't do. But most importantly of all, I couldn't summon my mother—couldn't even try to.

Broomie floated up beside me and rubbed me. As I went to pet her, I realized she was scorched down her shaft, too—had she been knocked unconscious as well?

"LAEH," I said quickly, and to my relief, she repaired, even the little bits of singed bristles regrowing so she looked as good as new.

I examined the room. Playing cards were scattered even farther around the house, a number of them blackened and singed behind me, where I hadn't directed any of my enchantments.

"The cards?" I asked, befuddled.

All I remembered was grabbing the salt and heading back toward the potions table, kicking some cards up, which went flying—into the fire.

"The tournament!" I shouted. "I *knew* there was something wrong with that old woman. We have to hope Cable stopped it—"

The town rang out with an explosion far, far more potent than the one I'd just experienced in here, the very ground beneath my feet rumbling through my stockings.

"No!"

Broomie straightened, as if in answer. I flung my hands out to where my hat had fallen off my head. "TAH, EMOC!" It soared to me and I flipped it on, just as I slipped on Broomie's back.

She rammed toward the door so hard, I had only a moment to shriek, "NEPO!" before we smashed right into it.

We soared up into the sky, into the night. Our destination was not difficult to discern.

"Fire!" I shrieked, pointing the way. In the heart of downtown, right where I knew Hungry Like a Pup and First Taste to be.

The tournament had started, despite my worst fears.

And the playing cards had blown up the place where much of the town was sure to be gathered.

Broomie soared, the wind whipping against my face like a barrage of little daggers, but I leaned forward, my heartbeat somehow both so loud and so slow in my ears, as if this moment were being stretched on forever.

The volunteer fire department would be mobilizing, but Roan and Abdel were among its members, and they were likely at the scene of the conflagration.

No, it was a witch's help Luna Lane needed most. Power boost or no, I *would* see the flames extinguished.

The shouts and cries grew louder as I neared downtown, residents making their way out of their homes to gawk—and in most cases, already making their way down there. I rushed overhead, practically clipping Spindra the spiderwoman as she ran down the sidewalk, stretching a thick rope of silk between her hands like taffy, perhaps ready to offer it in any rescue attempt. It would be useless while the blaze still roared.

"Dahlia!" screamed Roan from in front of the pub, his voice wracked by coughs. Beside him, Qarinah cowered on the pavement, covering her head and trying to make herself small. Vampires recoiled at large, uncontrolled fires. They were both covered in soot.

Broomie screeched to a halt and looked about to lower me to the ground, but I shook my head.

"We'll do this from up here," I said, gulping. No time to check the rest of the forms for familiar faces.

"NIAR!" I said, my voice thundering. I could feel the power I desperately grasped on to channeling from above me and down through my hat to my very bones. "SEMALF ESEHT HSIUG-NITXE, NIAR!"

The sky cracked with a bolt of lightning I hadn't asked for, and the screams below grew louder, but I held my arms out toward the burning pub, my left arm so heavy and itchy and irritated, it required every ounce of strength I had to keep the enchantment flowing in the overwhelming heat before us.

But it worked, the sky parting overhead just where we were, the clouds sending down torrents of rain.

The fire crackled and sizzled, and more figures slipped out from the pub's front door, Roan moving forward to assist them in getting out and away from the fire, away from my unnatural storm.

Panting, I tried to check on who was who out of the corner of my eye. Jeremiah. Todd. Erik. Chione, letting her grandfather lean up against her, his wrappings singed and loosening as he stumbled to his knees. Ingrid, with Goldie and Arjun supporting her on either side. She was coughing the worst, her hair half-singed.

Doc Day was on the pavement behind us, her boarder, Jamie, calling for the injured to make their way to her.

My heart thudded. But there had to be more.

A howl broke out, then choked as if the creature had gurgled a mouthful of rain, and out soared Grady, his one unmangled arm far too hairy—as if he'd somehow transformed partially into the werewolf he wasn't due to be yet. In his arms, he cradled Fauna and Falcon, and just behind him stumbled Faine, her beautiful red polka-dot dress half-mottled with ash. Flora was slung over her shoulder.

That left…

"Where's Cable?" I shouted, though I wasn't sure anyone could hear me over the rain I now directed to the last of the flames in the back of the pub. "And Draven? Anyone else?"

"Bette!" shouted Ingrid.

Oh, yes, Bette. No doubt perfectly fine if she'd engineered the whole thing with her explosive playing cards.

The fire sizzled out completely with a snap and I lowered my hands, my limbs so heavy, but especially my left one. I couldn't have lifted it if I tried.

Broomie brought me down to the ground and I slipped off.

"What about Cable?" I spun on Ingrid.

"He was running late," she said. "He wasn't there."

Relief flooded my entire body, only to be morphed into a strange sense of panic. Where *was* he then? Wasn't he supposed to stop this tournament? Or at least be careful with it? And stop by my house to get me before it had even begun?

Never mind that for now, though.

"Draven?" I asked, looking over the crowd.

Qarinah shrieked then, clutching her hands tightly over her ears, and my chest squeezed like a vise. Draven's instinct would have been to huddle in fear, too, rather than leave. It had probably been Roan's fast thinking that had gotten his girlfriend out of there.

The quizzical looks on their faces said it all.

"Lia—" started Roan.

I bolted inside, ignoring Roan's incessant cry of my name.

The stench of something like barbeque hit my nostrils almost immediately, charred among the thick smoke. It clogged my lungs.

"ESREPSID," I started, but I choked. Broomie shifted so her brush blocked my mouth. "ESREPSID EKOMS!"

The wreckage became much more manageable to navigate without the sizzling and the smoke.

I could fix the tavern—though I'd probably need a potion boost. But first I had to get him out.

"Draven?" I cried out.

The furniture was charred, a beam overhead crashed diagonally to the ground. Soot covered a mural at the far end of a Transylvanian castle, the speakers that would play out the low rumble of thunder melted like a runny egg down over the side of it. The selection at the bar was smashed, the medley of alcohol bottles behind it no doubt having contributed to the flames. There were several cracks running through the mirror, and I startled for a moment to see so many ghastly reflections of my face. The pain of the day was written all over it.

From the pattern of black streaks, I found the epicenter of the explosion, right where the tables had been separated for multiple euchre games the night before.

There was no sign of—

Some distance away from the blast was a charred corpse. I stepped back from the sight of it, my shoulders curling forward as my legs grew unsteady beneath me.

A flash of every positive memory I'd had with my vampire love passed before my eyes, slowing time down, down, down. All the fights, all the snobbery, was meaningless.

I couldn't say how long I stood there, just blinking.

Broomie tugged in my hand.

My mind was slow to consider what she wanted, but then there was the squeaking.

"Draven?" My instincts recognized his high-pitched little animal wail before my mind caught up to it.

Broomie slid from my hand and flew up, as far from the explosion as she could, to the place where two walls met the ceiling and a support beam met another to curve into a little crevice just wide enough for a bat.

A bat!

I raced over there, lifting my arm up so Broomie could give me a boost.

"Draven?" I said to the little thing. He was breathing hard, his fur covered in ashes, his wing bent at an awkward angle. There was a tear in the delicate membrane.

Every breath seemed to come with a squeak.

"Draven," I said more gently, extending my free hand. It crackled with the movement, the stone scale still sore on the inside of my arm.

One of his beady black eyes opened, and a sudden sense of lightness filled my weary body. Whatever was wrong with him, I would heal him. I just needed to get him out of here.

"Draven," I said again.

His claws, which clutched so strongly to the splintered beam, loosened one at a time. He crawled forward into my palm.

I bent my arm to swaddle him against my chest, and Broomie lowered us back to the ground.

"Lia?" Roan called out from the open doorway.

"Let's go," I whispered to Broomie, my gaze landing on the charred corpse across the room. On closer inspection, I realized it was too small to have been confused for Draven.

"I found Draven!" I cried out behind me to

Roan, though my eyes didn't leave the petite person who was beyond even the capabilities of all magic.

Something white and small caught my eye.

It was... a playing card clutched tightly in the charred corpse's hand.

A completely undamaged, bright white playing card.

I moved closer, and Draven whimpered against my chest.

Before I could blink, I'd snatched the card into my hand, black ash snapping off the person's flesh.

It was the ace of spades.

And though I would have pinpointed the cards as the cause of the explosion, it was perfectly unblemished on either side.

Chapter Eight

"I can fix it," I said, probably for the dozenth time this evening. "I can fix it —I just need... I need..."

"Rest?" Draven, back in his vampire form, sat with me on the steps leading to town hall. Inside, everyone was a buzz with what had happened during the tournament. Sherriff Roan was down the block in his office, making calls to his friend at the coroner's in the county.

Three months, four dead bodies. Even friends in high places might start having trouble pulling strings.

"I'm going to get home," said Faine, standing, but not before giving me another hug. "The kids must be so anxious."

I gave her hand a squeeze and she frowned at the sight of my new stone scale but didn't say anything.

By now, she'd had an account of my day.

And I'd had an account of their evening.

The tournament had just started, the idea being three tables of four would play two to three rounds and declare the winning team the one that won two out of three. Then the winners from each table would come together to compete, whichever team scoring highest in several rotating rounds named the grand prize winning team.

Cable hadn't shown, but Ingrid had been sure he'd be on his way. So it had been Draven, Qarinah, Roan, and Bette on one table and Ingrid, Mayor Abdel, Chione, and Faine at another. Goldie and Arjun had been on standby until the two of us missing showed up—or would take the winning team's place after for their own shot at the grand prize, even if that gave one losing team an extra chance.

Other Luna Lane citizens had been there to watch, including Grady and the kids, and Todd had stayed on for the night shift so someone could run the bar, at least until one or more vampires was out of the game.

Neither table had declared a winning team for two out of three hands yet. They'd only played about ten minutes before the explosion.

I just hadn't uncovered exactly *how* it had gone down.

"You hug them tight for me," I said to Faine. Those poor kids were already working through their trauma at Falcon having gone blood mad a couple of months back.

Faine patted Draven's shoulder and he gave her a tight-lipped nod before she headed off, down the direction of her home.

Behind us, the door to town hall opened, the artificial light so bright that even I squeezed my eyes in reaction. Draven couldn't stand it—it wasn't deadly like sunlight was to him, but there was a reason why he preferred places with dimmer lighting.

Chione stepped out, taking the couple of stone steps down to join me.

"Grandfather's resting. Finally." The mayor didn't live in town hall, but I knew he hadn't wanted to go home after I'd seen to his wrappings. His flesh had been in a state of decay by the time I'd gotten around to him, but thankfully, his wrappings had responded to my spell and mended. "Is he healed now?" I asked.

"Yes, thanks to you." Chione smiled, though it was fleeting. "All the damage done has been repaired, but it took a lot out of him. He could barely stand by the end of it."

"Join the club." I gestured to myself. Without any power boosting potions, I'd done a number on myself putting out the fire and healing everyone afterward.

At least I *had* been able to heal everyone afterward, not forgetting any internal damage from smoke inhalation.

Everyone except... Bette.

Despite my suspicions that she'd been behind it all, it was she who'd charred to the death in the fire. The only casualty.

"The playing cards sparked a smaller explosion at my house," I told Chione, as she hadn't gotten the full story from me yet.

Beside me, Draven traced an icy, pale finger over the surface of the stone step between us. The step was cold on my legs even through my dress skirt, but Draven wouldn't have been bothered by it.

"The playing cards?" Chione's nose wrinkled. "How? Why? Is that why you didn't show up at first?"

"Yeah." I rubbed my stony arm, flinching. The hard flesh had absorbed the cold just as the stone beneath us had. "But what I don't get is why you didn't stop the tournament—or at least wait for me to show."

Draven and Chione exchanged a look. Chione spoke first. "Well, we assumed you were coming..."

"There wasn't going to be an easily dividable number of players. Ingrid thought we could rotate and play losers against losers once you and Cable showed up, or maybe convince someone in the gallery, so to speak, to lend a hand." Draven swallowed noticeably. "The two of you gone—*I* assumed you were together. I should have waited for you. I should have known something was wrong—"

"It's all right. But I mean, Cable was supposed to tell you all about Eithne. He was supposed to come check in on me before the tournament, actually, but I'd have to assume he never showed."

My blood ran cold.

"Eithne?" Draven asked, his brow furrowing.

"The witch who cursed you?" said Chione. "Who's had her hand in everything that's gone wrong in the past few months? She was targeting the tournament?"

"Not exactly, so far as I knew, but I saw her yesterday." I turned on Chione. "Didn't Cable tell you?" Draven would have been asleep before sundown; I could see why the visiting professor might never have gotten around to spreading the word to him.

Chione shook her head. "I never saw him all day."

I jolted to my feet. Of course. Even if he *had* been running late, he would have been here by now. Considering our conversation this morning, he wouldn't have left me alone like that all afternoon to begin with.

"What is it?" Draven asked.

"Where's Ingrid?" I looked up at the town hall, but she wasn't among the people who'd gone there. She'd been so distraught about Bette… "We need to find Cable."

Draven muttered something under his breath.

I turned a sharp eye on him.

Broomie's prickly snore from behind us on the step above drew all our attention.

"He has to be with his mother," said Chione, though the color drained from her already tired face. "He was probably with his uncle to begin with. Perhaps he doesn't know what happened."

"I heard what happened from across town. He'd know."

Chione and Draven held a silent conversation across from me, as if I weren't even there.

"What?" I said curtly. "What is it?"

Draven rubbed the back of his neck, the tip of one of his fangs protruding to gnaw a little at his lip. There were bags under his eyes, and I knew he was overdue for a feeding, especially considering the events of the night. "I *did* feel strange starting without you and Cable. Not that I cared about Cable being there." He mumbled the latter part a little quieter.

"Me, too," said Chione. "I knew you were a bit reluctant to participate, but Cable organized the whole thing. And I thought you'd show regardless. You're one of the founders of the Spooky Games Club."

"Well, then why did you start?" I asked.

"I don't... I don't know." Chione blinked rapidly, her long eyelashes almost a distraction.

"Ingrid said Cable would show," said Draven. "And you… You…"

"Bette said not to worry about you," Chione added.

Of course Bette had. Nice to know the instant dislike I'd felt toward her had been mutual.

"I haven't spoken to Bette since last night," I snapped. "I mean… I didn't speak to her. I only met her that one time."

So she—and Ingrid—hadn't been worried by my absence or Cable's. Ingrid and her own son didn't make a lot of sense, though I supposed I didn't know their dynamic. She'd raised him around the world. Perhaps that had come with a lot of personal freedom to the point where she'd think nothing of her son being late to an event he'd helped organize.

But no. From everything I knew about Cable, he wasn't the type to be late. He took his responsibilities very seriously.

"How did the playing cards explode?" Draven asked. "At your house?"

"What?" I asked, massaging my temples. I needed to find Ingrid and speak to Cable—no, vice versa. I was so exhausted. "I kicked one into the fire."

Chione and Draven did that silent conversation thing again.

"*What?*" I tapped my heel against the stone step below me.

"Bette had a lighter," said Chione.

"We were in the middle of the game," added Draven. "Spades was the trump suit. I told her it was a no-smoking establishment."

"That's how I noticed," Chione added. "Since I was at the next table over. But smoke makes me queasy." A shadow passed over her face—she'd gotten more than enough smoke tonight. "So I looked over when Draven said that."

My head was woozy. "Did she put up a fit about it or something?"

"Not exactly, no." Draven hissed, both fangs protruding from his mouth. "She juggled the jack of spades in one hand, the lighter in the other—"

"The *jack* of spades?" I pointed out. "You don't mean the ace?"

"No." Draven nodded, lost in thought. "No, I'm sure of it. The ace of spades was the upcard of the trick."

The rules of euchre were still indistinct in my mind. "You mean, she wasn't holding the ace of spades."

"No. Why would you ask that?" Draven cocked an eyebrow.

"You didn't see." I let out a harsh breath. "You were too scared, I suppose." Draven flinched at that, though I'd found his little bat self curled up against me more endearing than his usual, hostile defensiveness. "Bette was clutching the ace of spades. And it was perfect. No damage from the fire at all."

"That doesn't make sense. She was holding the jack of spades. She was about to win the trick."

"Maybe you were mistaken?" said Chione.

Now he rounded his sharp, red-rimmed steel gray eyes on her. "I most definitely was not."

She shrugged. "Memory can be faulty."

"Not *mine*." He stuck his nose a little in the air, reminding me too much of his vampire sire, Ravana. "She was on my team. Of course I was watching what she was playing."

A sigh escaped my lips. I wanted to know *how* the fire had started, but it wasn't important just now. "So she lit up anyway, and things went boomy-boom?"

Both Chione and Draven stared at me, eyes blinking, for that. I was tired. It wasn't funny, with the trauma and the death and all the damage, but I wasn't trying to be funny. I just needed... I needed... I scratched at my new scale, my throat dry. When was the last time I'd eaten or even drunk anything?

Draven licked his lips. "She had the lighter and her cigarette in one hand, then she took a drink from her glass—almost spilled it, it was so full. I found that odd since none of *my* staff ought to serve a drink like that, especially something strong like straight vodka, which I'd heard her order. We always leave at least a quarter of the glass empty. I should have noticed it was too full as soon as she was served, but I didn't." He frowned, as if wondering which employee to chastise, but he continued. "I remember my hand darting out to protect the cards on the table from the spill. She laughed at me for that because she didn't spill a drop. I originally thought maybe the alcohol had caught fire. But come to think of it, she drank it all, throwing her head back for a single long chug before putting the glass down and trying to play her hand while she went to tuck the cigarette back in her purse. She said something like, 'Lighten up, sweetie.'"

"I think it was, 'Lighten up, *sweet lips*,'" added Chione.

The vampire's lips pursed and he stiffened. If Draven could blush, he might have. He was embarrassed about being hit on by an old woman? Didn't he know how very attractive he was?

Of course he did.

"She didn't smoke yesterday," I said, remembering. There'd been no argument about lighters, no scent of cigarettes wafting over from her.

"I suppose not," said Draven. "But I wasn't playing." He crossed his arms tightly across his chest, like he was jealous we'd been doing anything without him. *He'd* chosen not to participate in the practice rounds.

"Did she smoke after I left?" I asked Chione.

Chione frowned. "Not inside the pub, anyway. I think?"

"She better not have," Draven muttered. "She

claimed not to know about the rule when I brought it up. She was going to put the lighter away, but she wanted to play her hand first. She took the jack of spades out, slipped it in the same hand as the cigarette and lighter, and I don't know… Things are blank after that."

"Maybe the card flicked the lighter on," said Chione. "It was kind of big, wasn't it? Gold, square —I remember that red jewel on the front. It looked old-fashioned. Maybe there wasn't a need to hold a button when you flicked it open."

Red jewel? I definitely would have remembered seeing that.

The details permeated my mind, as my amateur detective abilities whirred into motion. I could almost picture the scene, down to Draven's minute observation of the card she'd had in her hand.

"Okay, so fire and playing cards. Makes sense. Someone can figure out where those cards came from, and we might have a lead." I nodded, the edges of my vision growing dark even in the dim light of the overhead street lamp.

"Do you think someone wanted Bette dead?" Chione's voice was a whisper.

"Or did Eithne play a role in this?" offered Draven.

I frowned. "Why not both? Maybe Eithne wanted Bette dead." I giggled despite myself. I almost felt drunk. "She *did* know about witches, after all."

"Dahlia, are you all right?" Draven asked.

I brushed him off. "I want Cable," I said. I'd meant I wanted to find Cable more than anything, but it was like a slap to the vampire's face.

His furrowed brow smoothed, his full, succulent lips thinning. "You need to rest."

"I want. To find. Cable." I poked Draven in the chest with every other word. His bare chest was cold, smooth.

My scalp felt itchy, and I realized with a start as I rubbed a hand through it that it came away dotted with dried, congealed blood. I must have hit it earlier during my own explosion—thankfully, the scalp felt fine, the wound or bruise I hadn't even known about healed with my enchantment.

Draven's mouth opened with a hiss, his fangs heading straight for me.

"You have to *ask* her—" started Chione, but her voice was drowned out.

Chione let out a little shriek behind me and Broomie shot up from her sleep with a shaking of her bristles, but they both felt so far away.

All that was real was the sharp piercing of Draven's fangs in my neck.

111

Chapter Nine

*M*om's cuckoo clock rang out, and though my eyes were practically crusted shut, my mind was waking up. I counted the bird's cries. Two o'clock.

Sunlight lit up my eyelids.

Two o'clock in the afternoon?

I shot up and groaned.

"Whoa, you gave me quite a fright!" Goldie shrunk back in a chair beside my bed, her hand clutching a cornhusk she was in the midst of feeding to Broomie. Broomie stopped chomping and chirruped, zooming over to rub my face.

There was a bandage over my throat that my fingers scraped as I moved my hand up to pet her, and the night before all came back.

"Draven," I said through gritted teeth.

No *hello* for Goldie. No asking her what she was even doing here. Just the vampire's name.

"Yes, about that." Goldie reached over to my bedside table and passed me a note.

It was written on older parchment, the paper thick and imperfect. Scrawled across in broad, black ink was a note from the vampire in question.

I am so sorry. I know you may not forgive me. But I was weary after the events of last night and your blood had been tempting me for a while before that moment. I haven't been drinking enough as of late, and in a moment of weakness, I… Well, you know the rest. I owe you my life after last night, and I will never be able to repay you. Yet now I owe you more for dining on you without your blessing. I am sorry. If it's any consolation, I feel you really needed the rest.

I crumpled up the paper and tossed it at the foot of my bed. Of course he'd slip that in there. That he'd done it for my own good.

Oh, that vampire was infuriating, and yet I couldn't let him go. Not entirely. Thinking him dead for a moment last night had made that clear. We'd be friends to the end, albeit somewhat awkwardly— and *his* end might come sooner than expected if he kept this up.

Rubbing at my itchy neck, I pointed at it. "LAEH," I said. I could feel the puncture marks I didn't even have to see to believe knit together and smooth out. The itchiness in my neck at least was gone, so I ripped the bandage off.

"What did I miss?" I asked. "Where's Cable?"

"Now, Dahlia, you had quite a day yesterday, from what I hear. Though you did a wonderful job

113

of cleaning up your home, so I couldn't have figured it from that."

"I used enchantments," I said, flexing my left hand and studying my arm. The skin still prickled as it moved, and I felt this sort of heady feeling, like something was weighing down my very blood. Probably the last traces of vampire venom, the stuff that most likely had been used in an enchantment to curse me. "My runes circle is still damaged. I'll have to… I'll have to repair it. It's not as simple as taking a knife and carving the symbols. I'll need ingredients from the woods, an enchantment placed on a sharp object…"

Goldie frowned. "But you'll have to complete your good deed for the day first." She took my left arm from me and turned it, wincing. "I saw this when I cleaned you. It's… It's awful, dear."

"And the next scale could take my whole arm out of commission, at this rate." I ran a hand through my hair. It was clean, not sticky. Goldie must have really done a thorough job of cleaning me—my friends had helped a lot when I'd been unconscious as of late. I couldn't cure or clean myself when I wasn't awake for it. I flung the blanket off and started shifting my legs off the bed.

"How'd I get here?" I asked. "Draven?"

Goldie nodded. "And Chione. She drove you over in her grandfather's car. I was at the sheriff's and I volunteered to go with."

"Oh. Thank you—I'm sorry you had to stay with me."

"Don't be silly," she said. "I was happy to."

I frowned. "But they found you at the sheriff's? We were at the town hall last I knew."

Goldie grimaced. "Draven turned himself in— for drinking blood from you without your consent. Roan just about clocked him, but Qarinah calmed him, blamed Draven fasting so much lately on top of the evening's awful events."

"So that's it?" I slapped my bare soles on the ground. "He gets off scot-free?"

"Well…" Goldie grimaced. "He agreed to serve a jail term. He's to report to the sheriff's office every sundown for the next month, going home only to sleep in his casket. Mayor Abdel agreed. I suppose that's as close as we get to a judge and jury around here. Don't usually need to try people and come up with sentences…"

I chewed my lip. That sort of felt excessive— only because if he'd asked, I might have let him drink from me, considering everything. Only I… I would have insisted he wait until I'd—

"Where's Cable?" I asked sharply, the details of last night unscrambling as that thought weighed heavily on me.

"Dahlia. Your good deed comes first." Goldie averted her gaze for a moment but then jumped up. "Oh, and food! Your stomach's been rumbling for ages." She jumped to her feet.

"*Goldie*," I said, harsher than I'd intended. "You're too obviously avoiding the subject."

Goldie wrung her hands. "He's missing, Dahlia. No one's seen Cable since yesterday morning."

Shell-shocked, I let Goldie practically stuff some naan in my hand before she plated a scoop of rice and soaked it in curry. "*Eat*," she said harshly, sliding the dish in front of me and serving up the same for herself.

We sat across from one another in my small kitchen, the tiny two-seater table just enough.

Goldie had tried to get my good deed out of the way for the day by asking for my help in preparing the food, but I hadn't been able to move.

"*But he warned you!*" I'd said. "*You were his first destination. Didn't he ask you to bring Broomie some cornhusks yesterday?*"

"*Warned me?*" Goldie had asked.

"*About Eithne! To keep an eye out for her, maybe cancel the tournament.*"

Goldie had shaken her head. "*He never stopped by Vogel's yesterday. As for the cornhusks, our bucket got full, and I just thought to bring it over. I saw you weren't home, so I left it on your doorstep.*"

So Cable hadn't been able to warn a single soul after I'd told him about Eithne.

I'd told him… and then he'd vanished. In broad daylight. At some point between my house and Vogel's across the street.

And I hadn't heard a thing, hadn't felt Eithne up to no good.

"EMOC, DRAWDOOW ELBAC!" I raised both arms above me as I spoke, fighting against the excess weight of my left arm. It was not the first time I'd tried this enchantment. Nothing happened. My fingers felt warm, tingly, like the magic was there and trying to get out—trying to complete its objective—but nothing came back as a result.

Goldie watched me expectantly.

"Nothing," I said, my arms collapsing against the table, my left arm landing hard with a *thunk*.

My brain searched for the words I hadn't tried yet, some enchantment that would put an end to this nightmare, but every time I closed my eyes and reached out to the ley lines of magical energy that surrounded Luna Lane, there was a distinct wall—and not just the one that kept me cut off from the rest of the world.

An artificial blockage. Something weakening my power, something keeping Cable from me.

What else could it be beside Eithne?

She was my only suspect. I didn't know why, exactly, she'd taken Cable, other than perhaps she'd wanted that tournament to go on. And she'd been watching me. Always watching me.

"If there's nothing you can do, there's nothing to be done," said Goldie simply. "Dahlia, eat."

I did as asked, if only to get through this monumental task and move on to the next thing.

I needed to be out there. I needed to be here, performing enchantments. Gathering ingredients for my potions—something. *Something!*

First Taste and probably even Hungry Like a Pup needed fixing, but I was too numb to take that first step.

And my good deed for the day. Oh, always with that good deed.

"Everyone's looking for him," said Goldie softly. "Everyone's worried. Ingrid is beside herself. Arjun had to tell her to stay home, watch Milton—he's confused again, and all this activity around him is distressing him."

"First her friend and now her son." My voice sounded like a croak.

It was more than I'd said in quite a while, though, so it almost made Goldie smile. "Yes."

Broomie was curled up at my feet under the table, the tip of her handle over my toes in a protective gesture.

My rumbling stomach responded aggressively to its first taste of food in over a day, but I needed it. I needed this over with.

With an energy I didn't know I'd had, I scarfed down the rest, stuffing my mouth with another slice of naan and washing it all down with hot tea.

"Let me talk to Ingrid," I said, slamming my empty mug down.

Goldie was only halfway through her own bowl, at some point stopping to stare at me incredulously as I'd put it all away. "Dahlia Poplar, you're not helping Cable until you help yourself. Good deed." She pointed at my forearm.

Gently, I nudged my broomstick off my feet, careful not to wake her if she needed the rest, and pushed my chair back from the table. I headed for my coatrack, where someone had hung my witch's hat and my shawl. "I'll help with Milton," I said stubbornly. If I had time.

Goldie frowned and quickly took a few more bites, leaving all the dishes spread out on the table and my counter. "I'm coming with you."

Broomie woke with a start at Goldie's loud voice and shot over to me, landing in my hand. "All right," I called back to Goldie, but I was already down the walkway and headed next door.

I approached Milton's house, taking note of Cable's tan smart car still in the driveway, and knocked harder than I'd intended—harder than I should have around poor Milton.

But Ingrid seemed as eager to answer the door as I was to have her open it.

She ripped it open, the cheer that usually dotted her expression replaced by pinched features, as if a weight were stretching all of her skin downward.

"Dahlia? Do you have any news?"

"I was hoping you did," I said, pushing my way past her inside.

"Ingrid?" Milton's deep, crackling voice sounded from down the hallway, in the living-room-turned-bedroom his wife had set up for him a few years back. "Are Mom and Dad back yet?"

Ingrid frowned even more. "No, Milt!" she shouted down at him. "They won't be back for some time." To me, she said, quieter, "He's not having a good day."

"Ingrid!" Goldie skipped up the front steps and stepped inside after me just before Ingrid shut the door.

"I take it you told her?" Ingrid asked her.

Goldie nodded.

We stood there in silence for a moment, just looking at each other. I wondered if I looked as exhausted as they both did. I sure felt it.

"I was the one who saw Cable last," I said, clearing my throat. Broomie's brush drooped at my words, her bristles giving off something like a coarse moan.

Ingrid perked up at that. "Where? When?"

"My house." I shirked under her studious gaze, though she didn't seem about to prod more. Broomie was wiggling wildly now, sticking her brush up under my shawl and poking through the gap around my neck to tickle the bottom of my chin, as if to show Ingrid and Goldie the coat-sneaking mischief *she'd* been up to the last time we'd seen

Cable. I nudged her brush down gently as I tried to keep speaking, figuring those details were better left unsaid. "He wanted to see how I was doing. I'd had a bit of a day the day before, and well... It was nothing compared to yesterday, in the end."

"A bit of a day?" Ingrid prodded. She gestured for me to follow her and we all sat down at the kitchen table, Milton's TV blaring some torrid argument complete with dramatic music from down the hallway. Broomie flew out from under my shawl as I took a seat, lounging across the kitchen island with her brush turned to the window overlooking Milton's backyard. The sky was overcast today, but she settled softly into the dim beams, two clumps of her bristles moving as if she were breathing out, "*num, num, num,*" before settling back into the nap I'd disturbed earlier.

I wondered how much she really knew about what was going on. She had an innate sense about what I felt due to our bond. She could respond to requests. But mostly, I just felt the warmth of her nearness, her need to let me know she was with me.

She'd always be with me. I'd never be alone. No matter what that witch did to me, no matter how many loved ones she took from me, there was at least that.

"I met Eithne in the woods two days ago," I told Ingrid, ready to reveal my theory on who might have taken Cable. "Do you know...?"

She nodded. "Everyone else brought her name

up, too. She was the witch here when I was growing up. Didn't much like the rest of us—stayed out there in the woods by herself. But we all knew about her." Ingrid grabbed a mug full of brown liquid that had been sitting on the table by its lonesome and sipped from it. It wasn't steaming, so perhaps her coffee had gone cold. She didn't look like she took any pleasure in drinking it regardless.

"Yes, well… She and I have a rather more personal history." I sighed. "She cursed me before birth—and she murdered my mom."

Goldie gasped. "You never told me she killed Cinnamon." Her voice choked as she ran a fidgety finger over a tassel on her shawl.

"It… I can't prove it, I didn't see it happen, but I saw her right afterward." I swallowed, pushing the image out of my head. Now was not the time. "In any case, she has it out for me—but she toys with me. She loves toying with people."

Ingrid grimaced and cradled her cold mug with both hands. "That was why Jessmyn and I were so scared of her growing up." I winced at the name of someone I knew Milton's wife, Leana, had killed in a fit of blood madness caused by Ravana. I wondered how much Ingrid knew about that. "It was said few would be willing to pay her price—and she was not to be trusted anyway."

"She was a character."

Everyone turned to see Milton shuffling into the kitchen from the other room. His soap opera was still blaring, but we must have held more allure to him. "Fun to be around. So long as you didn't get on her bad side." He shuffled past us without so much as a *hello* and opened a cupboard in the kitchen, fishing out a box of cookies and putting it on the kitchen island beside the curled-up Broomie.

She was *a character*? Did he even remotely remember her role in entrapping the souls of his neighbors and wife in a cursed board game?

Sure, it had actually saved their souls in the long run, but…

I was certain that had been an unintended effect.

I took a deep breath. At any given moment, Milton might not remember he *had* a wife, let alone that she'd died and a witch had played a role in the strange circumstances of her death and afterward. He could only remember witches existed half the time.

Ingrid and Goldie both seemed at a loss for words as to how to reply. Ingrid turned to me instead. "So you agree with Roan that maybe Eithne took my son?"

So I wasn't the only one who thought that. Duh. *I* wasn't the professional investigator here. "I don't know what else could have happened. His car is still here."

"But why?"

"I told him about her visit to me the day before. I was so busy trying to brew potions, trying to get to the bottom of her visit, I tasked him with warning the town and maybe canceling the tournament." I winced. "I'm sorry. I never should have put him in danger like that. I should have spoken up earlier—"

"And put us all in danger right then and there?" Ingrid offered. "Maybe she would have exploded us during the practice games. And then you would have been caught up in it and no one could have saved any of us."

Goldie licked her lips. "You think she caused the explosion?"

"Who else?" I ventured. We all fell into silence.

Milton was crunching his animal crackers awfully loud. I hoped his dentures wouldn't break. "But who did she do the job for?" he posed. He paused and petted Broomie's shaft gently, not even flinching when she came to life and stretched—so he remembered her today. She chirruped and rolled over so he could get access to another part of her shaft. He scratched her harder with a finger bent inward, and she twittered even louder, rocking back and forth. "She doesn't work alone," Milton said, stopping to pop another cracker in his mouth. "She takes jobs for a price." Broomie's brush jumped up as if to see why she wasn't getting a massage anymore.

His words cut through me to the core. But she *had* worked alone when she'd cursed me, when she'd killed my... No. Para-paranormal meant that

Eithne had at least had help when my mother had died.

Ingrid leaned one arm against the back of her chair as she shifted to look at her brother. "Milton, do you know who we're talking about?"

"Eithne," said Milton between more crunches of his crackers. "You've always been so afraid of her, Ingrid, but Dad's brought me to visit her more than once. Little fixes for the store, stuff like that." He gently batted Broomie's brush away as she slithered toward the end of the island to inspect the box he was snacking from. When she just pushed back, he fished out a cracker and offered it to her, but once she got a good look, she whipped her brush head back as if repulsed. Cornhusks didn't come in animal cracker boxes, but maybe she didn't know that. Milton shrugged and popped the cracker in his own mouth. "The witch of the woods. Eithne Poplar," he said between crunches.

Blinking rapidly, I settled the wave of nausea that overtook me. "Eithne Allaway," I said gently. It wasn't often worth correcting him and confusing him further, but I couldn't help myself. "I'm Dahlia Poplar. My mother was Cinnamon Poplar—Leana's friend."

Milton's gaze seemed to grow foggy for a bit. "Eithne Allaway... Cinnamon?" He stared at me, as if expecting me to admit I was my mother. We'd looked enough alike; I could hardly blame him.

Broomie looked between Milton and me, then

back to my elderly neighbor. The sudden tension in the air probably felt odd to her.

I couldn't answer. Tears pricked behind my eyes and a deluge of them just poured right out—silently, but not less potent.

Goldie patted my back.

"I'm so sorry," I said to Ingrid. "I wish I could… I don't know what enchantments to use to figure out where he might have gone. It's like my magic is blocked concerning him—and my rune circle is in need of repair. It'll take too much time to fix to be of much help." A deep breath escaped my lips and my next few words were quieter. "The last thing I wanted was for Cable to be in danger."

Broomie soared over with a little bristly wail and wrapped around my shoulders like a scarf or a very agile cat, being careful to keep her coarse brush a little distance away from the skin at my cheek. I patted her solid, wooden handle with my right hand as Ingrid reached across the table and laid a hand on my left, not even flinching when touching the stone scale. "I know that, dear." Tears pricked the corner of her eyes now, too. "Cable talked about you often on the phone—I know how much you mean to him. He wouldn't have wanted you to keep your worries to yourself."

Milton put his box of crackers back in the cupboard and shuffled out without a word. Displays of emotion in others made him uncomfortable since his dementia. He probably longed for the security of his TV.

"I'm sorry about Bette, too," I said, wiping my eyes.

Ingrid stiffened, but her face was still warm. "Now how would that be your fault? You tried to warn us. And you didn't bring the—was it really the playing cards?"

"I assume so," I said, quickly explaining what had happened at my own house the day before.

She grimaced. "Roan told me. Word got around fast."

"Whose cards were they?" Goldie asked.

Ingrid thought about it. "Bette's. Or at least... I was rummaging around in Milton's drawers and found a pack, but Bette had several in her bag."

"Several?" I asked. Broomie was settling back into her nap around my neck, letting out the repetitive, bristly sound I liked to think of as her snoring. "Yet she only had one bag, despite traveling the world?"

Ingrid looked toward the staircase. It was currently gated and closed so Milton wouldn't wander upstairs and hurt himself. "She traveled light, she told me." She shrugged. "I do, too."

"Can I take a look?" I asked.

Both Ingrid and Goldie stared at me.

"I've already been through it to look for any contact info for friends or family for Roan to use.

Nothing. Her purse, her phone, her ID—must have all burned up in the pub."

"'Must have'?" I ventured.

"It isn't like Roan's had time to do a thorough sweep," Ingrid said. "On top of dealing with the coroner, finding Cable has been top priority since I realized he'd never come home last night."

"It's just... Knowing why Eithne targeted the tournament—and if she actually had help, as Milton pointed out—might give me some clues as to what she's up to. Where she might have taken Cable."

"Mayor Abdel led a search party to the site where her cabin once stood," said Goldie. "Roan wanted to cover all the bases—and Eithne has had a hand in too much around here as of late, so of course she's on the list of suspects."

Just two days before, Eithne had brought the cabin back from the dirt and dust, so it was true that it might have served as a hideout. Too many long-living citizens of Luna Lane knew precisely where it had stood. They just hadn't gotten around to informing me of that before I'd stumbled on it on my own.

"Suspect *list*?" I asked curiously, focusing on what else she'd said.

Goldie shirked under my glance. "Well, I think she's the only suspect at the moment. And there isn't specific evidence to go on..."

"So it sounds like there's still a lot of work left to

do to solve this mystery, to figure out who put the Spooky Games Club in danger—and why." I wiped away the last of my tears, the cold stone biting against my cheek. "I need to help. And solving the mystery of the playing cards exploding—that's the best place I can think of to start."

Chapter Ten

There were four bedrooms upstairs, three of which had been occupied as of two nights ago. The bedroom Ingrid had led me to was stark and simple and it didn't seem lived in at all—though granted, Bette would have only slept one night in here. Still, she'd made the bed as if part of a military drill. I ran my finger over the plush blue wrinkle-free comforter, the satin white pillowcase not only devoid of blemishes, but without even a single white hair. It was as if she'd cleaned the sheets as well as made the bed.

Or she'd never slept in it at all.

"This was Milton's room, growing up," said Ingrid. She leaned against the open doorframe, her eyes scanning the room. "He used to have an astronaut poster right there."

I looked where she indicated and found the

faded gray dirt in the shape of a rectangle above the plain, wooden dresser, the pinprick holes at the four corners.

"The master is bigger, obviously, but Cable was already set up in it, and Bette said she didn't mind. She wasn't much of a sleeper."

"I'll say." I looked at the bed. "Did she sleep at all Monday night?"

Ingrid cupped her elbow and frowned as she examined the bed. Goldie shuffled in, taking a seat at the end of the bed herself. Broomie unwrapped herself from around my neck and joined Goldie, running her brush against the bed. The comforter crinkled immediately from all the contact, leaving a marked indent the moment Goldie stood again.

"Either she didn't or she's the type of guest who doesn't like to leave even the slightest hint of a mess behind," Ingrid ventured.

Bette's bag reminded me of a carpetbagger's. The gray fabric was rough to the touch, the flower pattern like that of a couch from several decades gone by—kind of like the one in my own house, actually.

The bag was open. Ingrid had already combed through the contents, as she'd said.

"Bette said you met in Salem, Massachusetts?" I asked her. "Hmm. No nightclothes."

I fished items out of the bag one at a time. A change of clothes—though only one outfit.

"Maybe she sleeps in the nude," offered Goldie.

Despite it all, I raised an eyebrow at her.

"What?" Her shoulder bobbed and she put a hand on her hip. "You don't have to be young and gorgeous to do that."

No comment.

Ingrid answered my earlier question. "Yes, we did meet in Salem. Last week. She was traveling alone, and we bumped into each other at the Witch Museum. We got to talking and had dinner together and I invited her on the next stop in my journey —here."

"Last week?" echoed Goldie, the surprise coloring her voice.

"Well, yes." Ingrid fiddled with her hands. "I often pick up a companion for a leg or two of my travels—it's quite common in the avid traveler circles."

Goldie's eyes were round. "I'd be too nervous, especially when it came to bringing a stranger to our town."

I didn't comment on the fact that she'd had Fred Beauchamp of all people in her house—though it had been her son who'd invited him and let him in on Luna Lane's secret.

Bette's bag held a jewelry box and inside was a simple gold chain with a red brooch. I frowned as I fingered the smooth surface of the jewel. It seemed familiar somehow. And not just because I remembered Bette wearing something—a gold chain, the rest of the necklace tucked out of sight—the night I'd met her.

"She already knew about the paranormal," said Ingrid, her posture slumping somewhat. "Otherwise, I never would have considered bringing her here."

The rest of the bag contained a tin of mints about half full. A "S'taffy Bar" candy bar in silver wrapping. Some dried flowers—a kind of field daisy, I was pretty sure they were. I used some in potions. And another deck of playing cards.

I gasped and set them down gently on the dresser. Goldie let out a little murmur and Broomie grew alert, stiffening and hovering behind me, as if ready to scoop me away from the site of danger at any moment. I signaled for her stay still.

"I didn't know about the explosive playing cards theory when I dug through her purse for Roan," said Ingrid, taking a delicate step back.

"I'll take them," I said. "Bring them home and see if there's any enchantment placed over them. I should really do the same with that ace of spades, too."

"Ace of spades?" asked Goldie.

"The card Bette was clutching when she died—though Draven insisted that card was actually on the table, that it was the jack of spades she'd been about to play."

Ingrid and Goldie exchanged a look. "I couldn't tell you," said Goldie. "I was getting a drink when the explosion happened." She rubbed her temples. "Arjun and I both—we were far enough away from it, close to the door."

"We all went flying," explained Ingrid. "Those of us near the explosion." I'd healed enough scrapes, bruises, and burns to attest to that. "I don't really remember more than that. It's like a blacked-out moment in my mind." She squeezed her eyes shut and shook her head. "If anyone has the card, it's Roan, I suppose."

"Right." Carefully, with both hands, I slipped the cards into the golden pouch at my hip. I didn't feel anything, no marked warmth or any off sensation, but that didn't mean there wasn't something off about the cards. Just that no one had cast an enchantment on them recently.

"Broomie," I said, gesturing for the broomstick to fly back into my hand. She did, though she was careful to stay at arm's length, away from the pack of cards at my waist. If I kicked the bucket, she did, too, but she clearly didn't want to be the one to jostle anything and put me in danger.

"Anything else you can tell me about Bette?" I turned to Ingrid, even looked to Goldie. She'd spent more time with her than I had.

"She had a dry wit," said Goldie. I hadn't asked her to *eulogize* the strange woman.

"She was friendly," added Ingrid, her voice breaking. "But I wish she'd talked about herself more. I might have had a clue where to begin when it comes to notifying someone."

"She was from Europe?" I asked.

"She said, 'the continent.' I didn't prod further. Now I wish I had."

"She grew up with witches and you didn't wonder exactly where?" Bananaberries. *I* should have asked her where. If she hadn't immediately gotten on my nerve, I might have thought more clearly.

"She didn't offer the information, and I don't make it a habit to pry into any of my companions' lives. It's kind of an informal code." Ingrid sniffed. "I figured she'd tell me more when she was ready. We had at least a few more weeks together before we might have parted ways."

I frowned. "But how did the subject of the paranormal come up between you? I get that you were in Salem, looking at a historical site important to witches—"

"That was it." Ingrid tapped her chin with one finger. "I guess... I don't remember exactly how we got on the subject of it all being real. I think I—no, I was being very guarded about it, no need to spread Luna Lane's secret too far and wide. Yes, it was she. She brought it up first."

"Bette did?" Goldie cocked her head.

"Yes, yes, I'm sure of it now. 'Burning witches, seeing if they floated—humans had no idea how to

135

really kill a witch.' That was what she said to me. We got to talking about witches, real witches—she seemed particularly interested in a witch's weakness."

Goldie gasped, glancing at me nervously out of the corner of her eye. Even Broomie let out a little chirrupy cry at that. She hadn't seen how Bette had acted around me.

What had Bette been up to? Hers was the only death—that we knew of… I sent out a silent, strong thought of hope to the ley lines for Cable—but had she really been nothing but a victim?

Was there such a thing as a witch hunter—and had the explosion saved me from finding that out firsthand?

"You don't think…" Ingrid laughed nervously. "She wasn't snooping so she could *kill* a witch. There's no way."

"You didn't see the way she practically ate me for lunch when she taught me euchre." The box of cards at my hip felt heavy, the sweat at the back of my neck reminding me I could be putting the whole house in danger. "Let me study these cards," I said, slipping by Ingrid. Goldie got up to follow me and I shook my head. "It's too dangerous for company."

I was out the door and headed for the stairs before she could object, Broomie vibrating in my hand and giving me a little hovering glide down the steps as she raised horizontally and dragged my arm above me.

"Your good deed!" Goldie called after me.

Right. Hours were ticking by.

But every moment I didn't have answers was another moment Cable was at the mercy of a callous witch who seemed determined to toy with me.

"Broomie, you stay here." I leaned my broomstick against my front porch. "Better yet… Wait by the end of the walkway. Stop anyone from coming in— and if there's another explosion, go get Roan."

Broomie wilted, her bristles scraping against the sidewalk in a sort of whimper sound. I tickled her under where her chin might have been.

"I'll be careful," I said. "But the best way you can help me is to stay out of the range of any potential blast this time."

She whimpered once more, floating away and then stopping to pivot her brush back toward me, as if to check if I'd changed my mind. I wriggled my fingers at her to encourage her, and she shook her brush against the walkway, sweeping the pavement in a sort of rebuking motion as she kept on moving away. Goldie and Ingrid both stood there at the end of the walkway to greet her, crossing their arms tightly and shivering, as if about to watch a controlled explosion from just beyond the edge of the blast radius.

Perhaps they were. I'd be prepared this time.

My rune circle was still damaged, so I didn't know how much help it would be in containing any explosion, but it was bound to be better than nothing at all. Crouching at the center of it, I carefully removed the box from my pouch. Taking a deep breath to steady my fingers, I slipped a nail under the seam and opened the box.

The cards so far had needed flames to explode —and there was no source of fire anywhere around me right now.

I could relax.

Sliding the cards out, I flipped them over, carefully shuffling through each card individually. Nothing seemed off about them. The red-and-green-patterned backs matched the ones Bette had used to play euchre Monday night, the ones she'd sent home with me.

The reminder made me glance around for any sign of *those* cards still scattered around the place.

Goldie or someone must have gathered them while I'd been out overnight because they were sitting in a stack on the little end table near the door, the empty box beside them. I'd have to test them, too, to compare. I already knew they were volatile.

I spread the new cards face down in the center of the circle then leaped to my feet, flipping through my mom's potions book. Power boosters were out of the question right now until I gathered more ingredients. But I had some dry, old stock of some basics. I might be able to…

Yes, page 103. *To Reveal True Nature.* It wasn't the most appropriate potion for the situation, but it was a very basic one. Normally, I could just rely on an enchantment for revealing a hidden truth. But I wasn't taking any chances when it came to the wrong words or a flick of my hand that would send the potentially volatile cards flying.

The only thing was… This potion required just a little bit of flame.

The cast-iron cauldron over a roaring fire for a large potion brew would be too risky. A little bit of flame would do. I could handle this.

Rummaging through my cupboard, I pulled out the dried fungus, the dehydrated St. John's Wort, and the sand that had absorbed some of a child's joy. I got that when needed from the sandbox in the Vadases' backyard. I put it all in an empty flask, and now it was the moment of truth.

Taking a deep breath, I pointed one little finger at an unlit candlestick. "EMALF," I said.

With a sigh of relief, just the one candle lit.

Taking hold of the glass with a pair of metal tongs, I rotated the flask over the open flame until the contents melted, browned, and bubbled, turning into a rich, mud-colored goo.

"All right." The words whistled out through my teeth. Impatient to wait for it to cool, I used the tongs to pour the substance over the face-down cards, then leaped back, outside of the rune circle.

Nothing happened.

Setting the flask beside the candle, I stared down at the cards, watching the potion disappear as it was sucked into the essence of the objects beneath it.

Nothing was revealed.

Were these cards not tampered with, then?

Taking careful steps toward the center of the circle, I crouched again and flipped over one of the cards.

The ace of spades stared back at me.

Strange for it to have been that card, considering, but there was nothing at all off about it. There weren't even traces of the potion left to discolor the bright white.

I flipped over the card beside it.

Ace of spades.

I blinked.

Then I flipped over the next card in the line.

Ace of spades.

My hands scrambling, all danger of explosion forgotten, I rapidly flipped over the entire deck.

Every single card—besides the original ace of spades, I had to guess—had transformed. An identical deck of fifty-two aces of spades spread out around my broken rune circle.

"What the…?" I stumbled back and landed on my rear. I didn't know what to do with that information.

With a rush of air from the dormant chimney and a rumble of thunder that cracked out across what had been a clear sky, the single lit candle flickered in the wind, crackling.

I jumped to my feet, my mouth open, but no words managed to escape in time before the flame jumped like a living, little being, lighting up candle after candle on the potions table.

Chapter Eleven

I braced myself for the explosion, but when the room beyond the stony forearm shielding my face was silent, I peeked out once more.

The flames were contained to the candles, the endless aces of spades still unmoved on my floor.

"Eithne?" I said, straightening my back to appear bolder than I felt. "Stop with the games! If you're here, come out."

But there was no response.

A bad feeling came over me. It was too quiet. Too calm.

No one had rushed in to check on me after that display of magic.

Running to the window in a panic, I poked my nose through the curtain.

Goldie, Ingrid, and Broomie were nowhere to be seen.

"No!" I sprinted to the front door and flung it open.

"Goldie? Ingrid? Broomie?" I ran to the sidewalk where they had once been. I looked left, I looked right. Had they gone back to Milton's? To Vogel's? It *was* chilly out here.

Fleeing across the street to Vogel's, I yanked at the door, only realizing with a start when it didn't budge that the "Closed" sign was hung in the window, that the lights were off inside.

Arjun would have gone out to help search for Cable.

I ran back across the street. They had to have gone back to Milton's. That was the simplest explanation. I should have checked there first.

I practically barreled into Doctor Day coming down the sidewalk, headed toward Milton's as well. She stumbled backward, her white lab coat swinging wildly open to reveal more of her bright floral-pattern blouse. She was clearly startled, but her face was alight. "Dahlia, you're better! So glad to see. Last night was—"

"Have you seen Ingrid or Goldie?" I asked. "Or Broomhilde?"

She frowned. "Goldie stayed with you. All night. Broomie was with her. As for Ingrid, I was about to come check on Milton and her both."

"They were all with me until… Never mind. They're probably inside." I ran up the walkway and pounded on the door.

Whoever was inside was taking too long to answer, so I whipped it open, Doc Day on my heels. "Ingrid?" I called out. "Goldie? Broomie?"

Milton shuffled out from his living-room-bedroom, his TV still blaring on behind him. "Cinnamon?" he asked, squinting at me.

Doc Day slipped past me to grab him by the arm. "Hello, Milton."

"Doctor," he said, smiling. "Hello."

"Milton, where's Ingrid?" I snapped.

Milton's eyes widened as I descended on him. Doc Day had to stick her arm out to stop me from grabbing him and shaking him.

"That won't help, Dahlia."

"If they're not here… They may have been taken!" My voice was louder than I'd intended it to be.

Milton started breathing hard, looking from me to the doctor. "Taken? Is my little sister taken?"

"Dahlia, you're scaring him—" started Doc Day.

"*I'm* scared!" I shouted, slipping to my knees. "I can't do this. Goldie… Ingrid. I can't keep… What am I supposed to do without Broomie?" I swallowed.

Broomie was supposed to always be here for me. My sweet little broomstick was supposed to make it so I'd never be alone.

Would Eithne stop at nothing? Until she'd taken *everything* from me?

Milton was moaning now, muttering his sister's name—and then his wife's again. Doc Day soothed him and guided him into the other room.

I didn't know how long she'd taken to settle him down, but at some point, I blinked and she was leaning down, holding out a hand. Her lips were in a thin, grim line.

"I called Roan," she said. "He said to bring you to the station."

The phone kept ringing at the sheriff's office. If I didn't know better, I'd think the news of all the goings-on in Luna Lane had leaked to the outside press, and everyone around the globe was calling for comment.

But it was easy to tell from the nature of Roan's short, curt responses that it was members of the town's many search parties all checking in—and not a one had a glimmer of good news. Now Roan had to inform them that we were looking for Ingrid, Goldie, and Broomhilde, too.

The door to the street whapped open and in ran Arjun, clutching at a stich on his side. "What happened?" His wide eyes moved from Roan to me and back. In the open holding cell behind us, Doc Day was speaking softly to Milton, who'd just about jumped out of his skin at Arjun's entrance.

"I don't know," I said simply. "They were all

waiting on the sidewalk for me to examine some playing cards and then—"

"Playing cards?" Arjun grimaced. "Didn't someone tell me *that* was what caused last night's explosion?"

"That's why I was examining them. They were in Bette's bag. Something was off about them."

"What exactly?" Roan put his hands on his hips and huffed. "We haven't had two seconds since you got here for you to tell me what."

"I'm not sure." I frowned. "But I have a theory about the card Bette was holding."

"Card?" Roan blinked. "Oh, right. It's in evidence." He gestured toward a filing cabinet. "Wrapped it up before the city boys and girls came to lug the body away."

The phone rang again, and Roan took a deep breath before going to answer it.

Arjun skidded to a stop in front of the desk at which I was seated. "What do the cards have to do with my Goldie's disappearance?"

"I don't know. But Eithne took her and Ingrid and Broomie, just like she took Cable. I'd bet my bottom dollar on that." At this rate, she would take half the town before I managed to uncover any more leads at all.

"*What?*" Roan's sharp voice garnered all of our attention, even Milton's on the cot in the cell behind us. "How is that even—You're sure? You checked the tapes? I... Okay. Right. Right.

Thanks." He slammed the phone on its cradle, his voice having offered very little gratitude at all.

"What?" I said, my heart thumping. Had they found them? Found... them hurt? Dead?

"Oh, it's not..." He flicked his fingers before cradling his head, as if fighting off a massive headache. "It was my coroner friend. Bette's body is gone."

"*Gone*?"

Roan sighed and took a seat in his office chair, the leather squeaking beneath him. "I'd say someone stole it, but they checked the surveillance tapes and swear there's evidence of nothing. She was there on the table one moment, and then she just... vanished."

"How?" asked Doc Day, removing her stethoscope from around her neck and tucking it into her medical bag.

"Your guess is as good as mine!" Roan threw both hands up in frustration and leaned back into his chair. "All that's left is a silhouette made of charred skin and ash. Promised me they'd run some tests on it. Not sure what good they'll do at this point."

"Eithne," I said under my breath.

"She's kidnapping corpses now?" he posited. "Out of town, I might add?"

"It's not like *she's* confined to Luna Lane," I pointed out. "She must have been somewhere all these years she didn't bother poking her nose into our business."

Roan leaned forward and drummed his fingers on the desk. "So… how can this help us? Where do we go from here?"

All eyes turned on me—as if *I* were the lead investigator here. I *was* the one with the most—or *any*, really—magical experience.

"I…" My throat felt dry and I licked my lips. "I can cast more enchantments over those cards. Figure out more about them, whom Eithne might have worked with—"

"Find her accomplice and make them cough up the goods on the whereabouts of our witch? It's better than any lead I've got." With a groan and an audible snap of his knees, Roan leaned on the desk and stood up to rummage through his filing cabinet.

In a large plastic bag was a bunch of black, fetid ash—and a perfectly unblemished ace of spades card.

"This the card you're looking for?" He shoved the bag across the table to me. Arjun jumped back. I didn't blame him. That card could have been explosive—though it had survived through the fire just fine.

"What else is in here?" I held the bag up and watched the crispy black flakes dart around inside.

Roan waved as he took a seat. "Her effects. A purse. Phone. All charred beyond recognition." The office phone rang again and with a heaving sigh,

Roan answered, the conversation back to the somber exchange of bad and worse news he'd been having with the search parties.

Arjun peered over my shoulder at the bag, as if he could find Goldie's whereabouts with a bagged clue.

"What's that?" He prodded the bag.

A glint of silver—charred at the edges—poked through and I shifted the contents aside to take a look. "Just looks like the edge of a candy wrapper." My stomach clenched at the disappointment.

A candy wrapper. Like in Bette's bag, too. Where had I also seen a candy wrapper just like this one…?

A pain shot up my arm and I let out a scream the likes of which I don't think I ever had before. The evidence bag fell from my fingers to the table and I moved to clutch my left hand.

The skin on my palm was searing hot, itching as if bitten by a thousand red ants.

"Dahlia?"

Any one of them could have called my name. Roan had hung up the phone and Doc Day was moving closer.

But their voices all seemed muffled, distant behind my pain.

Gazing at my palm, I watched as the flesh turned gray, then bright silver, the stone spreading outward and toward my fingers.

"No, no, no," I said, clutching my hand into a

fist. The joints creaked against the effort, but they bent—just not all the way.

"Dahlia, your good deed?" Roan spoke through rasping, shaky breaths.

I'd forgotten. After everything, after every reminder. I shook my head and bit down on my lip.

That was Eithne's aim.

Make me forget. Keep me distracted, worried for my loved ones.

Do whatever it took to finally turn me into the stone monster she wanted me to be once and for all.

Chapter Twelve

 he shooting pain subsided, though my hand continued to itch, what little pink flesh remained between yesterday's new scale and today's a bright shade of red.

The door behind me opened.

"May I come in?" Draven's voice was sullen, hoarse.

This wasn't a place of residence, but I didn't know exactly how the vampires' rules of invitation worked.

"For your sentence? You bet your biscuits you can come in." Roan moved around the desk and headed toward the door.

I shifted in my seat, Arjun patting my shoulder in consolation as I found my arm grabbed by Doc Day and she began an examination. As if she could prescribe anything that could help me.

"Dahlia?" Draven blinked as he approached. "What is... What happened?"

The thin, haughty line of his lips curled into a frown as he bent on one knee to stare at my scaled arm.

I chuckled darkly. "A new scale." I flexed the hand and Doc Day let it go. There was limited movement, the joints coated slightly in the stone. "But that's the least of what you missed while you were sleeping."

Draven stood and looked to everyone else for an explanation, but they all just looked tired. Roan sighed and shuffled some papers on his desk.

"Cable, Ingrid, Goldie, and Broomie are missing," I said, since no one else could speak. "I think Eithne took them."

Draven blinked. "How? When?"

The door opened behind him and Qarinah stepped in, a beautiful fluffy coat buttoned up to her chin, though the cold wouldn't have bothered her. Her grim lips became even more sour as she took note of Roan's haggard appearance. "Darling?" she said, quickly flitting across the room to slide in beside him. She directed him to his leather office chair and then the two vampires just stared at us, waiting for us to catch them up.

Between Roan and Doc Day, they got apprised to the situation—down to the latest detail about Bette's corpse's disappearance.

"So what now?" Draven asked grimly. He

searched the room's inhabitants for answers, but he found none.

What now indeed.

The phone rang again and this time, Arjun jumped on it. "It's Abdel," he said quickly, then he turned back to the conversation. "He found…" His eyes widened. "He found Goldie's shawl on his way back into town. I…" He let the phone slip back to the table. "I have to meet him out there."

"Arjun, wait—" I started, but he was already out the door.

Roan grimaced and picked up the phone, finishing the conversation with Abdel. He hung up.

"There's nothing for Arjun to *do*. The shawl was in a bush near your house, Dahlia. It could have flown off when she was taken. It doesn't really tell us anything we didn't already know—and there's no other sign of anyone."

The sheriff's station fell to silence once more.

Goldie had been taken because of me. There were no two ways around that. Eithne could teleport ghosts, we knew that much. No reason to assume she couldn't have teleported Goldie, Ingrid, and Broomie clear across the globe, leaving the shawl behind just to torment me.

Draven sighed. "I'll help—if you want me to. If not, I should get going on this prison term."

Really? He'd help if we *wanted* him to? Of course it was more helpful to have him out looking instead of sitting like a lump in a cell.

I found myself growing incredibly irritated that everyone had decided his "sentence"—for a crime committed against *me*—without my input to begin with. Maybe that wouldn't be enough to make me forgive him. Maybe he didn't even need to be forgiven, considering everything.

Sure, those were completely opposing thoughts, but I couldn't make sense of the jumble of my thoughts if my life had depended on it.

My vampire ex shuffled past me and the sheriff's desk and made his way to the single holding cell. "Or maybe the cell is too crowded? What are you in for, old fellow?" Draven crouched before Milton, a sense of warmth flooding the vampire's features.

Milton smiled warmly—so he didn't remember Draven's connection to Ravana at the moment, as any thought of the vampire woman who had driven his wife and friends mad was certain to upset him.

"I'm not giving blood," he said, shaking a finger.

Draven sat down beside him on the cot. "Don't worry, old friend. I know not to ask."

So Milton remembered Draven was a vampire at least.

The phone rang again and Roan scrambled to pick it up—but there didn't seem to be any news.

Doc Day shuffled back to the jail cell, calling out to Milton, and I followed, mostly because I felt like I wasn't done with Draven.

I'd gotten his letter, for one, but he hadn't apologized in person.

This martyr act by sitting in jail without consulting me wasn't worth half that.

"Cinnamon," said Milton as I approached. I twisted a lock of my hair around my finger, cradling my mostly-stone arm tightly to my side.

I didn't have the heart to correct him just now. It didn't even seem to matter.

"Is little Dahlia going to come make me laugh today?" He chuckled. "Last week, her auntie brought her over and she sang the 'Itsy Bitsy Spin-dra.' When I tried to correct her, she turned her button nose up and told me the spiderwoman taught her the *real* words."

My mouth gaped open as I looked to Draven and Doc Day for explanation. "My auntie? Spin-dra?" We were friendly, but we'd never been that close. I'd barely even spoken to her since I'd thanked her for my Halloween dress.

Draven shrugged. "I couldn't say. I stayed out of the witches' hair until you slunk into my bar on your twenty-first birthday."

"Except when trading kisses for an 'all in good fun' cursed board game," I muttered.

Draven's expression grew pinched.

"No, I think I know what he means," said Doc Day, picking up where Milton left off. "You don't remember?"

"My 'auntie'? Singing songs for people?" I shrugged. "Not particularly."

"One good deed per day," said Milton.

I rubbed at my left palm, my cheeks burning.

"It wasn't always chores," Doc Day said simply. "I assumed you just found them the most straightforward way to accomplish the task once you got old enough to take some charge of your situation."

I clutched the bar on the open jail cell door in front of me, almost as if for support. "What are you talking about?"

"*The itsy-bitsy Spindra went up Fifth Avenue. Down came the rain and wrecked her dress anew.*" Milton chuckled and kept singing, the words to the familiar song ringing in my ears.

"Well," said Doc Day, "when you were a baby or a toddler, your mom would just try to get you to make people laugh. But it had to be a genuine laugh —everyone wanted to help you, so we were eager to offer a chuckle, but it wasn't enough unless you really sparked unprompted laughter."

My fingers traced the smallest stone scales up near my shoulder. "I just thought I got a lot of extra scales when I was little because I wasn't able to comprehend the curse. But there were days when I succeeded in staving them away? Even as a baby?"

"It's true. It took a while for your mom to explain to you—and she was so worried about scaring you unnecessarily, but at the same time, it *was* important you pay attention to take care of yourself." Her eyes narrowed at the new scale on the palm of my hand.

"Little Dahlia has to feel like she's made a difference," said Milton, still humming his song.

"That was it. That's what she said." Doc Day nodded. "To stave off your curse, you have to feel like you've made a difference to someone—and sometimes, that could be accomplished with just a laugh. But as soon as she could talk to you about cleaning and chores and helping on errands, that just seemed easier. More likely to take. There were days when your mom was in tears because there was no way to tell you when you were a baby that you had to entertain those around you." Doc Day sighed. "A baby shouldn't have to worry about that."

"But why didn't Mom ever tell me? About the general 'make a difference' thing?" I was no Laurel or Hardy, but surely, I could work on my act and make people laugh on occasion. It'd be faster than doing a chore in a pinch.

"Cinnamon said the chores was a simple, guaranteed way to stave off the curse," Doc Day said. "But I didn't realize she hadn't told you about the entertainment aspect of it."

Letting out a deep breath, I realized the room had gone quiet behind me as Roan had finished his call. Now, *everyone* was watching me. "I wished she'd told me more. How did she keep my scales from growing in too big, for one?"

"Cinnamon had her secrets." That was Roan speaking from behind me. I looked and found Qarinah patting his shoulder, almost as if she'd heard his stories about my mom before. Perhaps she had. Mom was as close to an ex-girlfriend as the sheriff was bound to have had—only she'd never officially dated him. "Her life before Luna Lane being chief among them."

I tapped a foot. "I'll grant you that. But what would that have to do with my curse—"

"She didn't tell us about Eithne causing it. Any of us." He looked to Doc Day for confirmation and she shrugged, nodding. "Not for a few years anyway. Not until you were old enough to understand yourself."

What would that have to do with it? "I don't understand. What *did* she tell you I was up to when she wanted me to make you laugh, or why my little arm started sporting these scales?"

"She just told us you had to feel like you were making a difference or you'd grow a new scale," said Doc Day. "No one asked why—she was a witch, and she was so… Broken up about it."

Roan cleared his throat. "We all thought it was something she'd done to you herself—wittingly or not."

"*What*? Why would my mom curse me?"

"She didn't say it was a curse," said Doc Day.

"We didn't ask. Besides, don't witches think everything they do is an enchantment, not a curse?" Roan scratched his stubble.

Eithne's "enchanted game" instead of "cursed game." It seemed a minor quibble.

"Well, Eithne tells me most witches are even worse than her. And they're supposed to be up to mischief, not good deeds—the curse on me was a mockery of my mom doing good deeds for others."

"Maybe," said Roan simply. "Your mom was an angel—but she was already pregnant with you when she arrived. Whatever 'good deeds' Eithne may have been referring to, it would have had to have been during her life before Luna Lane if the witch really cursed you before birth."

"Not necessarily," I said, biting down on my bottom lip. "She could have cursed me in the last few months before I was born, after Mom got used to life in Luna Lane—"

"Dahlia, you were born the day after your mother moved here." Doc Day grimaced. "She never told you that?"

Chapter Thirteen

"No, I didn't know that." My hands clutched my skirt, only my right palm sweating, my stony left most likely blocking off any glands from expelling moisture. "Mom told me you knew her before I was born!" I looked to Roan specifically at that comment. He was like the dad I'd never known. He'd always been a part of my life. Since day one.

"I guess that's true..." Roan scratched at the stubble on his chin. "For one day. I greeted Cinnamon upon her arrival. She seemed so troubled."

Qarinah rubbed Roan's back, as if she knew more than he was saying. His inward gaze, his wistful, halting smile, made it clear he found the memory of Mom in distress painful even now.

"I didn't want to pry," Roan continued, "so I tried to distract her, get her off her feet—she was practically weighed down with every step, like she was carrying a boulder inside her instead of a little fiery-haired girl." He winked at me and I blinked rapidly. Had I been a heavy baby? "I gave her the rundown of the place. Frieda and Jonathan brought her over some supper from Hungry Like a Pup. Frieda was six months pregnant herself. They swapped stories. It went well at first, but then I remember Frieda complaining about morning sickness in the first trimester and Cinnamon's expression fell."

Huh? Had she had bad memories of morning sickness herself?

"By evening's end, she was laughing along with us again, though…"

"Though…?" I prompted Roan.

"When we went to leave, she was very keen on us not coming back again until the day after next."

The room went silent. All but Qarinah would have been in town at that time, but Draven had made it abundantly clear he'd never interacted much with my mom, and Milton's memories were fuzzy.

I turned to the town's only doctor since before I'd come into existence. "I was born the next day."

She tucked her hands into the pockets of her lab coat and gave a brief nod. "Abdel called me late in the evening and sent me over. I'd been busy while Cinnamon had moved in, so that was my first introduction to her—to you. But she'd already given birth by the time I'd arrived. She claimed she'd never called the mayor, that she'd managed just fine on her own, but she was kind about it and grateful for me to be there to give her and you an examination. The way she looked at you—the way her face lit up when I declared you a healthy baby—it was like you were the sun itself in a world that had long been deprived of it."

The gears in my head were turning, my arm weighing me down reminding me. "I wasn't strangely heavy?" I asked.

Doc Day and Roan exchanged a smirk. "No," said the doctor after a moment. "Seven pounds, six ounces. We don't get many infant deliveries in town since I send most mothers to the county hospital"—I nodded, thinking with a sharp pain how I'd missed visiting Faine in the hospital for her three kids' births—"so that measurement stuck with me. "

Well, it was good to know I hadn't been born the size of a boulder after all. Still… "She wanted to be left alone that day. She didn't even want the town's only doctor there! I know she had her enchantments, but… She seemed to know in advance I'd be born that day. And she didn't want any witnesses."

"Maybe she *did* expect something to be off about your birth," said Draven softly. "She knew how the curse operated—perhaps she was just relieved you came out with ten fingers and ten toes."

"So Eithne cursed me long before Mom arrived

here. She *helped* my mom move here, despite cursing me?"

None of this made any sense.

"Or," said Draven gruffly. "Maybe their original theory makes more sense. Maybe it was your mom who cursed you."

"No." I stumbled backward, my back hitting a filing cabinet. "You're wrong."

Draven shrugged and stared ahead of him. "I didn't know her well."

"That's right you didn't—"

"But I *did* know Eithne. Better than your mother at least." Draven lifted his head in the air. "She wasn't pleasant and I could hardly say she *cared* whether the people around her lived or died, but she never caused harm on her own. Not without payment."

"Well, maybe she got payment for cursing me," I snapped, gritting my teeth together. "She was probably working with someone else when she killed my mother, too, so there's someone—someone paranormal—who had it out for my mom. Maybe I was just collateral damage, or a way to hurt her."

"Or your mother was ashamed to tell you if she had any role in it." Draven's hard, steel eyes locked with mine.

If it weren't for Milton still sitting in the cell with him, I'd slam the door shut on him right now.

"I need to speak to Abdel," I said. "Why did he call Doc Day—how did he know to, if my mom claimed she never asked for his help? Maybe he was there. Maybe he knows more about what *actually* happened."

"You can ask, but I did the same not too long afterward," the doctor explained. "He corroborated Cinnamon's story—claimed he'd never called me. He hadn't even had a chance to swing by her house to welcome her yet. It was New Year's Day, and the town hall was closed, so he was taking the day off from official business."

"Didn't you find that strange?"

Doc Day and Roan exchanged that knowing look again.

"We discussed it back then in private and decided it was none of our business," said Roan. "If she used an enchantment to sound like Abdel and ask for help but didn't want anyone to *know* she had—"

"Why would she do that?" I asked.

Roan shrugged. We were out of answers again.

"Who was your father?" Doc Day asked after a moment.

I felt everyone's eyes on me, felt the weight of being put under a microscope.

"I don't… I don't know. Mom would never tell me." My stomach was churning, my throat dry and the very edges of my vision going black. There was too much I didn't want to think about—and now wasn't even the time. "What does this have to do with anything? Our friends are missing!"

Roan sighed. "And Eithne, unfortunately, is our only lead. If this is all about *you*, then I'd say the more we discover about what Eithne wants from you, the better our chances of finding her and saving our friends."

"She wants me to suffer." I cradled my face in my hands, the cool stone scale of my left palm like an ice cube on my cheek. I let out a little yelp and then sighed, wringing my hands together. "That's all I know."

"Your mother should have told you more," said Draven quietly. "Whatever caused this in you—"

"'It was always in your blood,'" I said, quoting my mom during her last visit from the realm beyond. "'The k...' 'The ka...' 'The curse'!'" I shrieked.

Milton startled, his humming stopped abruptly.

I blinked rapidly, pacing the small amount of free space in front of the holding cell. It made sense. She'd expected me to be born stone, I was sure of it. I was heavy when I'd been inside her, and she'd gone to such lengths to give birth to me in secret. Had I not caused her morning sickness? Had it actually affected her and had been traumatizing for her? With a dreadful thought, I imagined throwing up pebbles or something equally heinous. "I can't believe I didn't figure that out when she said it." I was babbling now, processing. "I... I thought maybe she meant my blood ran with my capacity for bad deeds, for an enchantment that led to death—"

"Fred Beauchamp?" Roan asked. "But that wasn't your fault. At all."

"I didn't think that at the time."

"So you're saying… you were cursed before birth," said Doc Day. "Before Cinnamon arrived in Luna Lane. And yet she trusted the witch who had cursed her, who'd endangered her child, to find her a quiet home for the birth."

I wrung my hands again. The stone scale was hard to squeeze, like grappling on sleek marble and finding no purchase. "Well, I always thought that I was cursed *before* birth. Mom said as much. But what if… What if…"

"Whoever your father was, his genes alone cursed you?" offered Draven.

I'd been about to mention my mom's family, a curse in the bloodline of witches. I'd been so used to not having a father, it was odd to even consider him —whoever and whatever he may have been.

"Bette!" I practically bowled Doc Day over to get back to the evidence bag on the table.

Roan cocked his head as he watched me. "What are you doing?"

Prying open the bag, I carefully dipped my hands into the ash and removed the unblemished ace of spades, setting it down just as carefully on the table. Then I sorted through what was left. A melted phone. A charred small handbag. Carefully, I unclasped the metal fastener on the bag and removed the contents. A scorched wallet. A flimsy, holey cloth that might have once been a handker-chief. Nothing else. I attempted to unfold the wallet, but it was difficult, the once-oozing, melted plastic sticking together.

"We tried looking for her ID," said Roan. "It's all unrecognizable."

"Bananaberries," I muttered, slamming the wallet on the table. A bit of ash flew up in a poof.

"What *about* Bette?" Draven asked, standing in the open jail cell doorway.

"She thought... She thought I was part gargoyle." I laughed. "I hadn't even known gargoyles genuinely existed."

Draven and Qarinah's eyes snapped toward each other, as if something were clicking into place. "Vampire venom," they said as one.

"Huh?" I looked from one to another. "Draven? You told me vampire venom was used in witches' curses—or wicked-intention *enchantments* if you want to get technical." I tossed that comment at Roan.

I didn't want any of this "it's all in the eye of the beholder" nonsense.

"Yes," said Draven, frowning. "Witches almost never want it for the good of others, I can tell you that much. It's potent stuff."

I was getting nowhere with him. I turned to Qarinah. "But why did me mentioning a gargoyle make you both think of venom?"

Qarinah scraped a hand through her thick, dark

hair. "Despite the stories about demons trapped in stone, gargoyles are actually a kind of golem."

"Bette told me that, too." My lips pinched together. "So are they more common in Europe?"

"Of course," said Draven dryly. "They blend in much better among all the stone statues decorating the old Gothic architecture across the continent."

I frowned at him. "And the vampire venom?" I reiterated.

"Golems are brought to life by witches—either for a client, or for themselves." Qarinah sighed. "Under the vampire code, we are forbidden from seeking out one as a servant. They're too volatile, too difficult to control for our kind."

"Witches make the best mistresses," said Draven, nodding.

"So the second paranormal creature Eithne was working with to kill my mom could have been a gargoyle?"

"I'd hope not," said Roan simply. "Dahlia, can't you see? You said it yourself. Bette thought you were part gargoyle—"

"My *father* was a gargoyle?" I lifted my stone arm, fighting against its weightiness. "No, no, no. That can't be. Right?"

"Those stone scales would make a lot more sense." Doc Day fidgeted a bit under the weight of all the stares turned her way. "I know nothing about gargoyle biology, but if you were half-gargoyle, it would stand to reason that it would show up some-how." She gestured to my arm.

It was always in my blood. It was a curse—because it was something that could cause me harm—but there'd been no avoiding it.

Eithne hadn't cursed me?

Impossible.

"But… But if a gargoyle is a golem, a stone creature brought to life, and not, as you say, a frozen demon or anything *living*…"

"I've never heard of a golem procreating," said Qarinah. She looked to Draven for a contradiction, but he just shook his head. "It doesn't seem possible."

"It was to Bette." Crossing my arms tightly, I started pacing again. "And Eithne collected a large amount of vampire venom from Ravana in the decades before I was born—"

"You don't know she used that for anything to do with you," said Draven. *He'd* been the one to put the idea in my head.

"What else could it have been for?" I asked, frustrated that he might have a point. "What else has that witch been up to all these years that any of us knows about?"

"Any number of things—not in town," pointed out Roan.

I frowned. "But say it wasn't part of the curse on me—because it was never a curse *placed* on me to begin with." It would make a lot more sense for

Mom to have trusted Eithne enough to move here, to be *friends* even, if Eithne had never cursed me in the womb. But that wicked witch had to have played a role somehow. I just knew it in my core.

"You think she used Ravana's venom to bring your father to life?" Qarinah asked.

My eyelids fluttered. Was that what I thought?

"Eithne brought my father to life?" No. No, I was still wrapping my head around the idea that my father could be a living stone servant...

"Or she delivered the venom to the witch who did," said Draven softly.

"My mother?" My knees suddenly weak, I fumbled behind me until I found a chair, sinking back into it. "But why? And then she *fell in love* with it—him?"

"Apparently." Draven's mouth quirked slightly. "A lot of paranormal creatures fall in love across species."

His eyes burned with desire, and I had to look away. "But never a witch with a golem," I pointed out. "Or so you tell me."

"Not that we knew of in Transylvania, in any case."

My heart was thudding so wildly, I had to close my eyes and focus to quiet it down. Now was not the time to get angry at my mom for keeping this from me—to unravel precisely what had happened in the past. We needed to find Eithne now.

Unless she was always nearby, waiting—waiting for me to figure this all out. My skin pricked.

"But then... Then there might never be a way to break my curse." I rubbed my hand over my left arm. "If it's just a part of me... That would explain why my mom could never do anything about it."

"But why would your genes confine you to Luna Lane?" Roan asked, his voice cracking. "We have no history with golems or gargoyles here."

"And what happened to my—to him?" I asked. I wasn't ready to start picturing an imaginary stone beast as my father just yet. "Why didn't he come here with Mom?"

There was still so much that didn't make sense.

"What if he's... dead?" Roan asked.

Then that would at least partly explain why Mom had run to a little supernatural town in the middle of nowhere a day before giving birth.

And Eithne had helped her?

"There's no such thing as a do-gooder witch. If you'd ever met another witch, you'd know that."

"Were they running from other witches?" I asked aloud.

Out of nowhere, the sky rumbled, a peal of lightning flashing so brightly, it flicked in and out of the sheriff's station, snapping the electronics with a pop as the room fell dark, then silent.

Suddenly remembering how the candles had all lit in my living room right before my friends had gone missing, I bolted up, running for the sole ace of spades card I knew to be on Roan's desk.

"Dahlia—" someone called.

But I snatched the card and ran outside, into the blue light of the full moon.

Chapter Fourteen

"*E*ithne!" I shouted out to the sky, waving the ace of spades above me. "Eithne, if you're there, show yourself!"

The door to the sheriff's station opened and Roan, Qarinah, and Draven followed after me: the witch seemingly talking to herself and waving a card above her head. I needed to get away from buildings in case there was another explosion.

"Eithne, I know you were working with another witch to kill my mother!" I yelled. "I know about the gargoyle! Maybe... Maybe witches aren't allowed to have babies with golems. I get it. I get it now!" My voice cracked into the night sky, but all the answer I got in return was another jolt of thunder.

"Give them back!" I screamed. "Whatever you want from me—you can have me! Take me to the other witches, explode me, let me turn to stone— whatever you have to do. But give them back!" I was choking now, on my words, at the emotions all rushing at once to the surface.

Roan appeared beside me, putting a hand around my shoulder, but I shoved it off. The sky cracked again overhead.

"Dahlia, it's going to rain," he said. "Let's go back inside. We have to stay in touch with the search parties."

"No, you go," I said, pushing against him gently. "Just in case. But I don't think anyone's going to find anything. It's up to me now."

A howl broke out across the sky and I remembered with a start it was the full moon. Faine, Grady, and their kids would be restless. I hadn't even asked if one or both of them had volunteered to help search. I knew they would have helped when they could have, but I also knew their wilder instincts would be taking over as the sun had gone down, so they'd have gone home. Grady and I had reinforced the backyard fence after the incident two months back, so it ought to hold them. Still, if this were any other full moon, I'd be there with them to make sure it all went all right.

When I needed my best friend the most, she couldn't be here for me—and when she needed me, I couldn't be there for her, either.

I had to have hope that the howl was just a reaction to the storm. Storms made werewolves uneasy.

"Where are you going?" Draven called out as I passed him by.

I stopped long enough to snatch him by the wide open collar of his leather jacket. "You, come with me."

He arched an eyebrow but didn't need to be told twice.

Walking home became a trial as a torrent of rain flushed down from overhead. Without Broomie, I couldn't fly, and I couldn't levitate with my enchantments for long enough to make it home that way. Draven could have turned into a bat and flown ahead, but he sullenly stuck his hands in his pockets, his shoulders slouched, as he speed-walked beside me.

"Where are we headed?" he shouted, his blond hair darkening somewhat as it clung to his icy skin. "Your house?"

Nodding, I held the card out to him. "I need to run more enchantments over the cards."

Water droplets stuck to Draven's upper lip as his mouth thinned, but he just kept pushing forward.

By the time we got to my house, my dress clung to every inch of my skin, my witch's hat drooping. I stood on the porch and looked at Draven, as wet as a muddied rat and as grumpy as a kid shoved unexpectedly into a pool. Were it not for everything, I would have laughed.

"YRD," I said, waving my hands at him. With a start, I realized my left fingers struggled to project the magical energy on par with my right. But it was enough. I repeated the enchantment for myself and the two of us were dry when we stepped inside my home.

I almost enchanted the fireplace to life and then thought better of it with all those playing cards around, instead flicking on the light switch overhead.

Grimacing, Draven squinted and put his back to the overhead lamp by my couch. There was no electric lighting in the living area where the potions table and the rune circle were located. Fire worked far better with enchantments, so my mom had had the bulbs in the ceiling removed from the start.

I gently put the ace of spades in my hand down on the end table beside the stack of cards Bette had given me a few nights back.

"Any reason why you've collected nothing but aces of spades on your floor there?" Draven asked.

"Ask Eithne, not me," I snapped. Then I took a deep breath and explained what I had done to the cards to get them to change.

"So… Each card's true nature is an ace of spades? But why?"

"I… I don't know. I didn't have time to consider that. Unless…"

Draven tapped an elbow impatiently. "Unless what?"

"Bette was a cheat. Think about it! You swore she was holding a jack, not an ace—she'd have won the trick with the jack. And when I was playing with her, she won every hand—except for one. I noticed she seemed almost aggravated that Cable won that trick. Maybe she'd planned on changing her card to that same card he won with to win the trick again."

"And how would she have *changed* the cards?"

I gasped. "*She* was the other witch! She must have enchanted the cards to change to a proper euchre deck, but anytime she didn't have a good hand, she'd change her card to what she needed."

"But why start with a stack of ace of spades, then?" Draven asked. "Why not just change the genuine deck one by one as necessary? You have to buy fifty-two decks of cards to pull out fifty-two aces of spades. Seems like if she went to so much trouble, she was trying to say something with her choice of cards. What might that have been?" He gestured at the large stack of them.

"I… I don't know." I chewed my lip.

"And don't forget, if your theory is correct, there would be two of some of the same cards in play."

"Not if she changed whatever card she was hoping for to the one she had in her hand."

"But euchre uses a small deck. Players would notice the cards in their hands changing—"

"Okay, the theory isn't perfect—unless, unless…"

Draven's chin tilted down this time, as if waiting for me to continue.

"She changed the memories of the other team!" I blinked rapidly, more clicking into space. "Did you ever feel... I don't know, *lightheaded* during your game with her?"

Draven absentmindedly scratched at his throat. "I? I am often lightheaded. But..." He closed his lips tightly.

"But?"

"Well, now that you mention it, Qarinah complained of a headache at one point."

"Right before the explosion? Before Bette was about to win?"

He nodded.

Just like Goldie.

"I'd forgotten it after everything that happened afterward, but now I remember... It struck me as odd." Draven massaged his own temples. "Headaches are a constant companion for those of us vampires who haven't imbibed enough blood, but ever since she started courting the lawman, I would have figured she was well-fed."

A burst of adrenaline shot through me, some innate, deep sense of fight or flight trying to get my weakened knees to flee.

"What is it, Dahlia?" Draven asked. "What did you figure out?"

"I don't know about other witches, how skilled they may be," I said. "But I do know Eithne can perform enchantments without speaking them out loud or holding out her hands. And she can change memories. My mother couldn't do that. It's rare for a witch to be able to do that."

"So Bette was as skilled as Eithne, you're telling me?"

Was that what I meant? My heart was roaring in my ears. I was missing something still, I was sure of it. Did it have to do with the message in the cards, as Draven insisted the surplus of the ace of spades had to be?

When I didn't reply, Draven picked up the cards Bette had given me, the ones I hadn't examined yet, shuffling through them.

"Careful," I said.

"I *am*," he snapped back. This was just like when we'd been dating, and I'd gotten on his nerves. Which in turn had led him to get on *my* nerves. "Where did you get these?"

"Bette gave them to me after the practice game a couple of nights ago. Said I needed to practice more before the tournament." I snorted.

He frowned. "This is a full deck."

"Yeah? So?" I asked.

Draven counted under his breath. Always counting with him. "Well, it's missing one card… The ace of spades, no doubt not coincidentally."

I had no idea what to do with that information. "At least one card had to be the catalyst that started the mini explosion in here. So maybe that was the one I kicked into my fireplace." I gestured to the cold, ashen logs and put my hands on my hips, looking around the room, as if waiting for a clue to jump out at me.

"Yes, well, what I mean is, we were playing euchre that night."

I tossed my arms in the air. "Draven, you've lost me."

Draven's gaze flicked from my head to my toes and back again. "Don't remind me," he muttered. Then he focused on the cards once more. "We played euchre with a twenty-four-card deck, remember? It was the same when you played. That's fairly common. Sometimes you can use a few more cards, but you never use all fifty-two."

My hands fell to my sides. "Well, that... That's easy to explain. She had the extra cards in the box and then slipped the cards we'd been playing with into it."

"I suppose. Though you couldn't really practice euchre if you had no idea how many cards to use."

"Or have anyone to play it with." Gently, I extricated the cards from his hand and flipped through them myself. "Bette wanted me to have these."

"Because?"

"Because..." My mind raced. What did I know about the woman, her general unlikability aside? I'd found the extra cards in her bag at Milton's house. I realized with a start I was staring at my floral-pattern couch. Her bag hadn't just *looked* like my couch; it was almost like it had been made of the same material. I passed Draven, taking the few steps to my couch to run my still-flesh hand over it.

"Dahlia, now it is you who have lost me."

That necklace with the red jewel. A half-full tin of mints. A silver-wrapped candy bar. Dried field daisies. I recognized them from some potions.

In potions!

I scrambled back past Draven, so fast, a lock of his long hair went flying as I flipped open my potions book. "Potion for better sleep," I mumbled, reading one possible concoction out loud. That one strangely required straight vodka—not often an ingredient in a witch's potion. Well, we knew Bette hadn't slept, at least not at Milton's. "To boost tele-porta—" I stopped.

"Teleportation?" Draven finished for me. He leaned over my shoulder to read the book, the chill he brought with him sending a quiver down my spine.

"I tried this one," I said. "Just in case I could teleport outside of the barrier keeping me confined around Luna Lane. It didn't work, of course. I'm not even strong enough to teleport *within* Luna Lane." I kept flipping through the book, all the way from one end to the other, to make sure I hadn't missed any that might have used that daisy.

"What do these potions have to do with—huh, that design." Draven tapped on the inside of the book cover.

I froze. The Poplar family crest. "What about that design?"

"It reminds me of Bette's lighter. The one she had in her hand before…" He gestured to either side of him, an explosion sound effect escaping from his lips.

I scowled at him. He shrugged.

But then I felt my heart almost stop.

"Bette was… a Poplar?" I ventured.

"She never did say her last name," said Draven. Though it wouldn't have mattered if she had. She could have given out a false name. "Bette" may have been a false name.

That red jewel… To keep one grounded. Bette had been wearing a jewel around her neck—if the necklace I'd found in her bag was the one she'd been wearing the night I'd met her—that was just like the one my mom had given Ginny.

"Then did she come here to meet you?" Draven asked.

"Or kill me?" I added, remembering Eithne's warnings about the other witches. I would have taken it with a grain of salt, but there was the fact that Mom had fled here and hidden from the other witches—had trusted Eithne above all others she'd known.

"What an unpleasant family reunion." His snow-pale finger tapped a small black design in the corner of Mom's family crest. "That looks familiar."

I leaned forward. It was too dark in here to get a good look. "WOLG." Though my power flickered somewhat, my fingers lit up, and I held the light over the design. "What are you… A spade?" I asked. Why hadn't I ever noticed this before? It was small, sure, and perhaps I'd just mistaken it for an abstract part of the design, but now, with the ace of spades thrown in my face over and over, there was no mistaking it.

"A pike," Draven corrected. "An old weapon from the continent. An iron spike attached to a very long pole. But it is the basis for the spades suit in cards, though its other meaning is nobility, depending on the culture."

Nobility? I looked to Draven as I let the light in my fingers fade. "You know a lot about the origin of cards."

He tossed a lock of hair over his shoulder. "They were quite the sensation in the fifteenth century."

Right. Ancient man walking here.

"The Poplar crest," I said, tapping the spade— pike—design. "Nobility?"

Draven grinned. "Perhaps you are a royal witch."

"As if there were such a thing." My heart fluttered and I stared Draven down. "*Is* there such a thing?"

"Witches are very secretive," said Draven. "I have never heard of a witch queen or princess, but that does not mean that if they existed, they would let themselves be known by other creatures of the night."

So many facts and theories danced around in my head now, and I tried to connect them all, then push away the ones that seemed to be less helpful in my goals. Find Eithne. Find my loved ones. That was all that mattered right now.

My hand ran absentmindedly over my arm. "Let's focus on Bette," I said. "Now that her body is 'missing,' I have a bad feeling."

"She was working with Eithne?" Draven asked.

With startling clarity, I realized... "And she's not dead."

He let that one sit for a moment. "She let herself be burned to ash and then get dragged over to the city for processing, then... up and left?"

"Do you have any other explanations for why her body is missing? The daisies—she brewed potions to teleport out of the coroner's office. The sleeping potion, too! Perhaps she put herself to sleep so deeply, she would appear dead for a time. That might explain why she hadn't bothered sleeping the night before, since she knew she was about get a long nap and she needed to prepare. Oh, and her drink! She added something to her drink with all her sleight of hand, maybe hidden in that oversized lighter, and downed the potion in the alcohol right before the explosion. Of course! The sleeping potion even called for straight vodka."

"Then what sparked the fire, if not the lighter, which you are saying was used only to smuggle in a potion?"

I rolled my eyes. "Witches don't need lighters to start fires. An enchantment!"

Draven recoiled and frowned, as if trying to catch up. "But she was *burnt*."

"Burning witches isn't their actual weakness!" I shouted, Bette's own words coming back to me. "She said herself that wasn't how you hurt a witch."

"Still. That looked like it *would* hurt, even if it wouldn't kill her."

I had to admit he was right. I'd burned myself before on the stove and brewing potions. It had left marks—I'd just been able to enchant them away. "Maybe the sleeping potion would be enough to knock her out. Or maybe it didn't hurt *her*. From what I know just from Eithne and my mom, it's clear witches are capable of great magic. It just... skipped a generation with me."

"Don't be ridiculous." Draven went to pat my silver arm and practically recoiled at the feel of the hard stone beneath his fingers. Still, he soldiered on, giving me a squeeze I could hardly feel. "Whether you are a real princess or not, you're amazing, Dahlia."

"You're just saying that because you..." I snapped my mouth shut.

"Because I what?"

"That's not important." I forced out a cough as an excuse to tear my arm away. "Can we focus?"

Draven flinched back. "So... Bette's a witch who wanted you dead? Then why start the tournament without you?"

"Maybe she thought the playing cards she sent

home with me took care of the deed. No one else noticed me missing—but maybe she and Eithne were quite aware of what had happened here hours before."

Draven ran a hand through his hair. "I didn't think you'd *want* me to swing by your house before the tournament. I'd only just woken up beforehand."

I raised both hands. "I wasn't accusing you, Draven. You didn't do anything wrong."

One of his fangs poked through out his mouth as he chewed his bottom lip. "Not until later that evening."

I nodded, my eyes flitting to the floor.

"Did you get my note?" he asked.

"I did…" I left the rest unsaid. I wanted more than just a note.

"I'm sorry," he said, his deep voice throaty. "I never should have—even with everything, that's no excuse."

My voice strained. "No, you shouldn't have. But I may have agreed if you'd asked—"

"You were too worried about *Cable*." The name seemed unpleasant on his tongue.

That reminder stung sharply. His actions had kept me from finding Cable for even more hours than necessary. "Then you're right. Maybe I would have said *no*."

We were at a stalemate.

"I'm sorry," he said again—simply. His jaw

clenched slightly, as if stopping himself from saying more.

"You're forgiven," I said. "Don't waste your evenings in the jail cell."

"Roan—"

"I'll talk to Roan. Right now, there are more important things to deal with. And when everyone's back, safe and sound"—because I refused to believe there was an alternative—"I'll get First Taste back up and running for you, so you'll be busy."

Draven clasped both hands to where his love handles might have been if he'd had an ounce of excess fat and nodded curtly.

Then his focus shifted. "If Bette and Eithne wanted you dead, they would have made *sure* you were. But you weren't."

"Then they wanted someone else at the tournament dead as well?" I ventured.

"Yet they managed to kill exactly zero people, if Bette herself did survive? Doesn't sound like the competent witches you assure me they must be."

I strode over to my potions table, setting the stack of playing cards down between several flasks.

"WOLG." I shook my right hand in the air and let the simple, safe light guide me as I flipped through Mom's potions book again—starting with the harder stuff I hadn't yet reached in the back.

"What are you looking for now?" Draven asked.

"Another potion recipe," I said. "That's why I asked you over here, really."

Draven bristled. "And here I thought you just wanted me along for my good looks."

I rolled my eyes. His ego didn't grate on me so much now that we weren't dating, but it wasn't as amusing as he seemed to think it was.

My palms slapped against the page as I found it, on page 699 of 781. My fingers grazed over the title on the top of the page. "Potion for clarity."

Draven stepped closer as he read over the ingredients. Though a chill bit in the air, there was a marked absence of odor from him, and I remembered with a start how Cable smelled of old books and tea tree oil.

"Oil of magnolia, crust of moss," said Draven, his voice choking. "I can barely remember what it is to eat anything, but surely, you can't mean to ingest that?"

Tapping my finger on the last ingredient in the list, I stepped back from the book so he could get a closer look.

"Vampire venom." Draven grimaced. "If things weren't as they are, were you going to eventually ask me for this?"

Chewing my lip, I shrugged. Yes, when I got that far in the book. But I hadn't necessarily expected to ask *him* for it. There'd been two other vampires in town.

I shuddered at the thought that I may have asked Ravana, back before life had become topsy-turvy.

"Dahlia, I don't know if you want a potion that has anything to do with—"

"It says it's for 'clarity.' That doesn't sound so bad."

"But if it asks for vampire venom. I told you what venom is usually used for in witch's concoctions."

"But we've decided venom was most likely *not* used to curse me, if my curse is simply genetic. Will you help me or not?"

"What are you going to do?"

I stared down at the rune circle. Fixing it was beyond my knowledge—it wasn't a simple matter of saying "XIF" and waving my hands.

"Get some clarity," I said simply.

Chapter Fifteen

I left Draven to it—funneling his venom directly into one of my vials, which he assured me would be no easy task. He didn't want me to witness him at work. Just as well. I made my way to the woods at the edge of town and gathered some of the missing ingredients. The night was more than half over by the time I'd just about gathered all of the other ingredients I'd need for the potion. Fortunately, the few things out of season I had in stock, other than the peppermint oil essence, but that was a simple matter of heading to Vogel's across the street from my house.

Unfortunately, they were closed—and would be by this time on any day, let alone a day in which so many of my friends were missing.

Sending up a silent apology to Arjun and Goldie, wherever she was, I stood in front of the door to Vogel's. "NEPO." I waved my hands.

The lock on the door clicked and the door swung open.

The moonlight streamed in from the bright celestial body outside, throwing most of the darkened store into a silvery shade of light.

Arjun and Goldie didn't often let their customers do their own shopping—it wasn't forbidden, per se, but they'd rather keep you talking while they provided the service for you—so it took me several attempts to find the aisle with the oils and spices.

I'd left the door to the street open, and the whole store flooded with a blast of chilly November air.

"MRAW," I said gesturing at myself. A soothing sense of warmth flooded my body—everywhere but the left arm. I flexed my stiff hand uncomfortably as I gazed over the array of little dropper bottles.

"Oil of peppermint," I said, taking the small vial off the shelf and making sure to take note of the price.

Without my rune circle, it wasn't possible for me to summon money from the space between dimensions. But there was still those few hundred dollars Faine had forced back into my belt.

I pulled it out as I passed the front counter, but I froze as I held the bills in my hand.

They were paper. Just rectangular pieces of paper. White, wrinkled, somewhat shaped like cash, though the feel was different. There was writing on it, looping cursive, promising worth from the Bank of Ireland, but it didn't even resemble any euro or pound I'd ever seen online or on TV.

When…? How…? This had most definitely been proper currency when I'd put it in there.

As if I didn't have enough to think about. I thought immediately of Faine—the Mahajans, the vampires, the town hall. Anyone I'd paid with this currency. Was this even real money?

Stuffing the foreign paper back into the pouch at my belt, I looked around the empty space but found no sign of Eithne.

"Show yourself already!" I shouted. I held up the peppermint oil. "If you don't want me to achieve some clarity, then where are you? Stop messing with me and fight like a witch!"

The front door slammed shut with a rumbling, heavy gust of wind.

Grabbing on to my hat, the peppermint oil still clutched in my hand, I closed my eyes as a rack of candy bars by the cash register rattled, sending a silver-wrapped bar straight for my face.

The wind died down and the candy fell to the counter with a *thunk*.

I stared at it, this "S'taffy Bar." It sure seemed familiar. And not because I'd ever tried it before. Taffy-coated s'more bar, the back of the package explained. My teeth ached just looking at it. Sure seemed like it'd be too sweet.

This was the wrapper Bette had had in her

purse—and in her effects left behind in the evidence bag.

But the font of those letters. The "aff" was particularly recognizable. The wrapper I'd dug out of the remains of Eithne's cabin!

Still, I'd already known the two were working together.

There was something more to it. There was the spade again—the pike. Just a small, unremarkable part of the design in the corner, easy to miss once the candy was open and the wrapper torn at the edge.

Gritting my teeth, I snatched the candy bar off the table, took off with the peppermint oil, and swore I'd make good on what I owned the Maha-jans—whenever I got around to what had happened to my cash.

Bolting back inside my house, I found that Draven had locked himself up in my bedroom. My cuckoo clock struck five in the morning. He'd have to go within a few hours. I hoped whatever he was doing to extract his venom would be over before then.

I let him be and got to work. After a few more minutes, I had exactly two rose-colored power-boosting potions prepared, a single candle burning once more to melt the ingredients together, but I couldn't start the potion for clarity until I had every-thing ready to go. So it was time to focus on what else the cards might be able to tell me.

Carefully, I stacked the deck that had become nothing but aces of spades and put it on my kitchen counter, far from the candles and the fireplace, even if I only had the one candle lit. I wasn't taking any chances that Eithne wouldn't light them all again. I set the card Bette had been clutching slightly off to the side, lest I mix them all up.

Now I had to do what that conniving woman had likely wanted me to do all along—examine the deck she'd given me.

I brewed another concoction, leaving only one candle burning as I worked, this time putting together the potion that had worked before to reveal true nature. As that cooled, I spread out the deck I'd received from Bette, all face-up this time in the center of my rune circle—for what broken boost it might offer the enchantment.

Using the tongs, my left arm noticeably heavy, I poured the flask's contents over these cards. Impatient, I muttered softly, "HTURT RUOY LAEVER," spurring the potion's work along.

The cards fluttered, as if shaken by a gust of wind. Even the potion seemed to be having difficulty absorbing into the cards' surface.

I crossed the room to take a sip of the power-boosting potion and tried again, setting the vial back on the table beside me and sticking my tongue out because of the sour taste. "STERCES RUOY LAEVER," I said to the cards.

They shook now, on the precipice of transforming, but it looked like they just needed a little more boost.

Whatever enchantment was on these cards, it was strong.

I drank the entire power-boosting potion, only registering the candy bar I'd placed beside the peppermint oil falling toward the ground as I tossed back the last of the potion. I only just had time to swallow back the bile because of the sour-tasting concoction before the candy was sure to hit the pile of cards.

I didn't know why my brain told me the candy hitting those cards would be a bad idea—but that was my first instinct.

I tossed the flask aside, and it smashed against the wall with a crash.

"POTS!" I said to the candy. "YAWA EVOM!"

But that sent everything scattering—candy bar, cards…

The door to my room clanged open and Draven thudded down the hallway. "Dahlia, what was that crash?"

Two cards—both now aces of spades, I noticed, my earlier enchantment and the potion having worked, after all, despite my impatience—were flying straight for the single lit candle, the wretched candy bar heading the same way. I couldn't say why I thought of it, but the enchantment that escaped my lips was, "MROFSNART!"

I thought maybe if the cards had become pillows or something, nothing would explode.

Why had I left that candle burning at all?

"Get down!" screamed Draven, sliding across the room to grab me.

By the time he wrestled me to the ground, I registered a clatter and a clank, the breaking of glass, and a pop and a fizzle... But no explosion.

I blinked rapidly, Draven's strangely muted steel gray eyes blinking back. The red rim that typically surrounded his irises was faded, and there were actual dark bags under his eyes. The venom extraction had taken a lot out of him.

He hovered over my face a moment too long and I firmly put my palms on his chest to push him back. Sliding a hand through his hair, he looked around us.

No explosion, no fire, just a scattered pile of playing cards all over the room.

And a long, black, silver-tipped spear—no, pike, I supposed was the technical term, and the only thing that made sense—crossed with an equally long silver wooden staff.

"Where did those come from?" Draven asked.

"I..." I scrambled to my knees. "I think this is one of the cards—and the S'taffy Bar."

Draven's brow wrinkled. "What's a S'taffy Bar?"

"S'mores meshed with taffy, I guess. I don't know. But it was a favorite of Eithne's—and Bette's, if I'm not wrong."

Draven looked around at the room, at the throng of aces of spades flung all over the place.

"So you think Bette was trying to tell you something?"

My eyes darted to the other pile of cards on the kitchen counter. I had aces of spades coming out of my ears at this point.

I scrambled over to the weapons I'd produced with my enchantments. They felt solid—the pike especially heavy in my dominant hand, though strangely when I switched the staff with the pike, cradling the pike with my left scale-covered arm, it felt just right.

As if it added no additional weight to my arm.

"Is that onyx?" Draven asked, taking the bottom of the pike in his own hand.

"I guess," I offered. "Why?"

"Nothing, it's just… The material of choice for weapons wielded by gargoyles."

"You know an awful lot about gargoyles all of a sudden." I leaned both weapons against my potions table, surveying the damage, and finding a number of empty flasks shattered on the ground. "You didn't care to tell me these creatures existed when you saw the stone scales on my arm."

"I never imagined it had anything to *do* with gargoyles," he said. "They don't walk around with mostly flesh and just a little bit of stone scales like you do."

"But they're not half-witch, any of them." I sighed, looking at the weapons I'd made.

Over and over again, the cards had pointed me here—to a pike. An ace of spades. The pike—represented by the spade—is my ace?

And that candy bar. A staff. A staffy... I had nothing.

I'd had enough of riddles.

"Is the venom ready?" I asked, whirling on Draven.

He put a hand on his hip, jutting his chin out. "'Thank you, Draven, for spending hours squeezing your very vitality out of your bones,'" he said, mocking my lack of gratitude.

I arched a brow at him. "Thank you," I said simply.

He sighed. "You'll have to make do with what I got. I'm about to pass out." He shuffled down the hallway and returned a moment later, the vial half-full of a bubbly blood-red substance.

Gently, he placed it on the potions table, about as far from the lit candle as he could.

"Do you need a pick-me-up?" I asked, pointing to my neck.

His chest thrust outward, his hand back on his hip. "Don't offer me that."

I didn't ask. Maybe he didn't think he could stop himself. Maybe he knew there were more important things to worry about just now.

Maybe that level of intimacy was too painful for him.

For me... I felt as if I could handle it. I still loved him—but that love had changed, from intense euphoria to disgust to affection again. He could still annoy me, but it didn't matter so much when it wasn't my boyfriend getting on my last nerve. When it was just a friend.

I couldn't say all of that, though. His gaze turned away, his jaw clenching just slightly—it was as if my eyes had spoken for me.

Without another word, I approached the potions book and flipped to page 699.

I worked the potion for clarity silently, using a mortar and pestle to grind the thicker ingredients down, shaking the flask above the lit candle with the tongs from time to time to meld the ingredients into one. At last, it was time to add the venom. I measured it carefully, leaving at least a quarter of what he'd provided me in its own flask. I could only hope I never needed the stuff again.

When the venom hit the pale lilac concoction, the potion in my hand fizzled and sizzled before I'd even placed it over the candle. I jumped back and Draven let out a little grunt, but I held my arm out to him, keeping him at bay.

With the tongs, I brought the concoction over the flame, shirking back just slightly as the potion popped and flew outward.

"Dahlia?"

"It's fine," I said, though I felt less sure of myself than I wanted to be.

As the potion muted into a dark, deep purple, I watched, waiting for it to cool.

"You're sure you can drink——" started Draven.

He wasn't wrong. Potions to be ingested generally didn't include poison, and in its very technical sense, that was what vampire venom was. But now wasn't the time to overthink. I downed it before he could finish his question.

It tasted like copper—copper covered in garbage and peppermint. Whatever witch had written this book apparently could not account for anyone having a sense of taste.

I belched and clutched my stomach, letting the empty flask fall to the ground.

"Dahlia?"

I found myself in Draven's arms and I used him to steady my suddenly weak knees. I blinked, the room around me, though lit only by candlelight, suddenly coming into greater focus, no detail escaping my notice.

The rune circle kept drawing my eyes to it.

It was broken, weakened—not enough to summon my mother and get her to give me any clue as to where Eithne had gone.

But I knew where I'd been in an intact rune circle recently—if I just could trick the stronger witch into bringing it back for me.

"Dahlia?" asked Draven as I straightened, giving his arm a gentle pat.

"Go home," I said, snatching my shawl off the coatrack by my doorway and fluffing the ends of my hair out from under it. "It's almost sunrise."

"I can't just leave you—"

I clutched him by the hand, letting the cold of my left palm absorb the intense chill of his own flesh.

"I have to do this alone," I told him. "And you've done more than enough."

"Dahlia—"

As if to punctuate my point about sunrise, Mom's cuckoo clock chirped out into the house.

"Swing by Roan's if you need to do something for me before you head home," I said. "Tell him to hold everyone back from the woods for a while—but if I'm not back by the end of the day, you all should assume I'm dead."

Draven looked about to be sick. "What are you planning?"

I crossed the room and took the pike up in my left hand, the staff in my right.

"To end this."

Chapter Sixteen

*T*he trek to the little lake where I'd found the remains of Eithne's cabin was long without Broomhilde. The uneven ground was sometimes treacherous beneath my ballet slippers, and I found myself stopping to enchant them to transform into a pair of black leather boots, the suggestion planted like a clear, unavoidable bolt of lightning into my too-alert mind.

The weapons grew heavier as I trekked through dirt paths, fighting my way through bushes, brambles, and fallen logs, but I kept moving, finding my left arm capable of bearing the load of both weapons after a time.

The way there was distinct in my mind, the woods around me growing sharper, more defined, as the sun made its way over the horizon.

With startling clarity, I realized I might never see Draven again now—or anyone I'd left behind.

But the thought of Broomie, of Goldie and Ingrid—and with a rush of emotion, of Cable—kept me moving forward.

I would see my human friends once more, even if it was the last time, and see them back again safely.

With a heavy heart, I knew my death would mean Broomie's as well. But we'd be together in the end, if it came to that.

Though at last the lake was sparkling in the twilight beyond the canopy of naked-limb trees ahead, it was not my mind's razor-sharp insistence to prepare for battle that overtook me just then.

No, it was the whimpering—dog-like, but still much richer, much more potent—that stirred my feet forward, despite all the bleatings of warning echoing in the back of my mind like a cluster headache.

"Faine!" I pushed past the last bit of brush in front of me, even my sharp mind scrambling to come up with reasons for why she was here, for why she sounded like a dog—the sun was almost up, the full moon having set.

But there she was—a wolf, with the sun up. I'd recognize her tawny brown fur, her wild, big brown eyes, anywhere.

She curled up in the middle of the ruins of Eithne's cabin, whimpering and licking a back leg.

I skidded toward her, the weapons flung aside and forgotten.

"Faine?" I asked.

Her head shot up and she looked exhausted, her eyes squeezing together as if she couldn't possibly keep them open much longer. Her front paw was chained to a stake—the stake struck precisely where Eithne's rune circle would have been.

But Mayor Abdel had checked this place yesterday. I looked around. No sign of the others kidnapped. Perhaps she'd been brought here afterward. I'd been so mixed up yesterday, I hadn't even made sure she was safe at home, secure from the temptations of the full moon. Maybe she'd gotten out.

I couldn't ask her anything now, though, not that she'd be able to answer.

"EERF!" I gestured at the chain.

To my relief, it popped open and Faine, limping, rubbed up against my side and cheek, her soft fur tangling with my hair.

With a rumbling clarity inside me, I realized my newly made weapons were in danger and I turned, but the clear sky grew dark and a rumble of thunder sounded overhead. Faine whimpered and pressed harder against me. I hugged her with one arm, reaching behind me toward the weapons with the other.

But it was too late.

With a *whoosh* of air, the black broomstick that was Eithne's companion soared down from the sky and managed to balance both weapons upon her back before retreating off to the stone campfire circle a few paces away.

Eithne sat there on one of the stone seats, her legs crossed, her long, silvery hair flowing around her face in the aftermath of her broomstick's movements. She collected both weapons in one hand as her broomstick settled by her side.

Turning her gaze on me, her lips curled. "Glad to see my distraction worked, despite your attempts at clarity. You are so simple to predict, Dahlia Poplar. It'd be a waste of magic to hinder you."

After giving Faine a squeeze, I stood on shaky legs. I knew I was in the center of the remnants of Eithne's rune circle, but that, at least, was where I'd always intended to be.

Let her predict *that*.

"Why is Faine still a wolf? Where are the others?"

"Faine is a werewolf because I felt it would be more theatrical to deal with her this way." Eithne's lips puckered.

"But how?" I patted at Faine beside me, trying to shove her slightly back, to tell her without saying anything to get out of harm's way.

"Just a little magic by suctioning energy directly from the night's full moon." Eithne picked a piece of lint off the front of her pale lilac skirt. "But I don't imagine a half-witch like you could ever achieve such heights of power, so I won't bother you with the details of the enchantment. Just be grateful I settled on your dearest, oldest friend and not any of those cute little pups. Them I locked up in their basement, along with their father, and they'll stay as wolves, too —for as long as the enchantment lasts. Shame the town will have to miss out on their big dinner today."

I blinked. It was Thanksgiving. I hadn't given the holiday any thought in days.

"LAEH," I said quietly to Faine beside me and her leg grew sturdier beneath her, though my enchantment had no effect on her state. I hadn't expected it to.

I gently pushed at Faine again, and she got the hint, nudging me with her cold nose and murmuring a soft sound before skittering backward into the brambles. I held both my arms out in front of me in case Eithne got any ideas, but she shrugged.

"She's served her purpose. I have other pretties to keep you here." She stroked her broomstick with her free hand, and the black brush nestled around her shoulders like a cuddly snake. Then Eithne stood.

"You've always known about my father," I said. "That he was a gargoyle."

Eithne's eyes grew wide, a smirk working its way onto her features. "It took you long enough to figure that out."

"I didn't even know gargoyles were real!"

The sounds of Faine's quick, retreating footfalls

grew softer behind me and I felt at least one small sliver of relief.

"Your mother and I disagreed on what to tell you," said Eithne simply. She paced closer to the lake, dragging the staff and the pike with her, one in each hand. "I wanted to tell you the truth almost as soon as you could talk."

I clenched my fists together. "Don't speak as if you were friendly with my mother."

"You know I was." Eithne looked fleetingly over her shoulder at me. "Your mother confirmed that herself." Then she tossed first the staff and then the pike into the water, the splashes echoing out over her words.

The sharpness of my mind flinched at the loss of the weapons, but there was a confusing thought striking hard at the forefront of my mind—to let the weapons go beneath the waters, beneath the surface of the lake.

I couldn't have retrieved them just now if I'd wanted to. I had to stick to my plan. I was right where I needed to be.

"Okay, I'll grant you that. But if you were still friends when I was growing up, I would have known." I dug my heel stubbornly into the dirt beneath me.

"Not if we didn't want you to." Eithne turned and stared at me, her broom slithering out from around her neck and flitting into her hand. "Yes, sweet Broomholly," she said to her, stroking her shaft. "It's time, old friend."

"My mother wouldn't conspire with you—it makes no sense!" *Just draw the wicked witch over here. Get her to do her little cabin rebuild trick, renew the rune circle...*

"I agreed to play the villain," she said—and my heart thumped wildly with what felt like a sharp sting of clarity.

I wasn't detecting any lies, though that couldn't be how the potion worked.

"We thought if you had someone external to blame—someone other than your father, who of course wouldn't have hurt you intentionally—you could focus your anger, sharpen your skills for the battle to come."

My mouth floundered open like a fish's. This wasn't at all what I'd come here to hear from her.

"I don't know what you're talking about."

"Don't you?" Eithne was closer now, standing where her fireplace had once been. Her broomstick —Broomholly, I now knew—curled up on the broken hearth, and just like I'd hoped, Eithne waved her hands and the cabin started melding together.

I swallowed. Keep her talking, distracted—it was my only hope.

"The other witches," I said hoarsely. "You said my mom was an exception. That the others aren't good. You expect them to come after me? Like Bette did?"

Eithne put a hand on her slender hip and laughed. "Bette? Another witch?"

"But you…" My heart thudded, and I clutched at my chest, realizing with a start that the potion for clarity seemed to be making its way through my circulatory system, thickening my blood with the weight of knowing things too sharply. "The two of you were working together. Her *body* vanished—that was her teleporting, I figured that out. She brewed potions to boost her capability to teleport across the county, to put herself to sleep before the explosion at the pub. She's as strong as you. She's as spiteful as you. She even likes the same… The same candy…" My voice croaked.

I'd disliked Bette from the start.

She'd gotten under my skin like almost no one ever had—no one except Eithne.

"*You* were Bette?"

As the cabin finished forming, the last tile of the roof sliding into place just as the dirt beneath me grew into solid wood, Eithne gestured at herself, her skin wrinkling, her silvery hair pure white. Her simple witch's dress became a sweater and long skirt.

Bette stood in front of me—and then with another wave of her hand—became a walking corpse flaking off in ash.

Despite myself, I startled, almost losing my footing.

Eithne laughed, throwing her frightening head

back as she began shifting to her normal, beautiful young-looking self.

But this was my chance.

I jumped just out of the rune circle—she wouldn't trap me in here this time—and shoved my hands downward.

"RALPOP NOMANNIC, EMOC," I shouted. "REHTOM YM, EMOC!"

The runes lit up brightly, the ground shimmering with my enchantment.

And inside the center of the circle, without any difficulty at all, appeared my mother.

Chapter Seventeen

"*D*ahlia!" Mom was pale, a specter of what she had once been. She floated atop Broomhannah, her companion broomstick, who was equally as faded.

Mom's hair was up in a bun, the silver streak through the fiery red along with the slight indent of wrinkles at the corner of her eyes the only indication that she'd been older than me when she'd passed.

Eithne looked stunned for once, her mouth slack as her body stiffened. "You foolish child," she snapped. "Can't you see? This is the last time you can summon your mother from beyond—and you have *wasted* it."

So apparently, I wasn't so predictable after all.

Still, my stomach clenched at her words. The clarity pumping through my veins found no lie in them.

This… This was the last chance I'd have to speak to my mother for the rest of my life.

Mom blinked slowly, tears somehow coming to her eyes, even though she had no body to speak of.

I reached out, knowing the ghostly hand that extended to me could never touch mine.

With a heavy heart, I wished Broomie were with me more than ever, to say goodbye to Broomhannah and Mom.

But the clarity reminded me my time was short, and unfortunately, too much would go unsaid.

The shine glistening in her faded green eyes, though—I knew somehow she knew everything I wanted to ask.

I ignored Eithne as the duplicitous witch approached.

"Mom, was my father a gargoyle? Was that why I was cursed?" I asked.

Eithne froze and looked to my mom.

Mom smiled sadly. "He was—he *is*. He was my golem." She looked to the witch beside me. "Eithne procured the vampire venom I needed to bring him to life, right here in Luna Lane." Eithne looked away at that.

Ravana's venom! But why? Eithne had helped the wretched vampire drink half the town to blood madness so my mom could create a golem?

"Why did you need a golem?" I asked my mom.

She locked eyes with Eithne and I felt irritation

that this silver-haired witch was stealing some of the last moments I'd ever have with my mom.

"Mom, were you a queen?" I asked, thinking of Draven's silly theory, the spade in the family crest. Perhaps the golem had been a bodyguard.

"A princess," said Eithne. "Our mother is queen. Queen of all witches."

I stumbled, slamming back into one of the cabin's walls. "No," I said. "That isn't... That isn't possible. No one knows about witch royalty. And you—" The lucidity clicked into place. "*Our* mother?"

Mom looked down tellingly, too quickly. "My sister's and mine."

My throat was so dry, every swallow felt like little knives traveling down my insides. Mom spoke rapidly now, perhaps trying to shift the focus, or too aware of her limited time.

"My bodyguard and I... We fell in love. I wanted to set him free, so I did. By then, I was already pregnant with you."

"Did he know?" I asked. The words barely escaped my throat.

She shook her head, the tears falling now. "He couldn't know. It would put him in too much danger, and he was in danger enough as it was. And he would never have agreed to part from you. From us."

"He thought she was dead," said Eithne huffily,

crossing her arms. "I mean, long before she actually died."

There was a painful tightness in my throat at the thought of a person out there who didn't even know he was a father—*my* father. And how did a golem work exactly? She could free him, and he'd still exist? From all I'd heard about the creatures, before I'd known for certain they were real, they faded back to clay—or stone, as it may have been—when their masters had no need of them. But the sense of clarity kept me focused. Those were questions for another day.

"Mom, did you lie to me, then? Eithne never cursed me?"

Mom shook her head. "No. Eithne's been watching over you. She planned her escape from the coven years and years before I did—and she was much smarter about it. She amassed the money we used to survive."

"*Eithne?*" I spun on the silvery witch, who looked away pointedly, her button nose in the air. I yanked the strange, old paper that should have been modern money out of my pouch. "The money I summon is from you?" I blinked at the paper. It was American currency again.

Eithne laughed and the money flickered back into the old "Bank of Ireland" notes. "I cast an enchantment so it'd transform into the currency you use. It's probably worth far more than the modern dollar, merely for rarity's sake and collector's sentimentality, but I figured if you saw what it really was, you'd ask questions. I'd hardly think the old currency devastated little Luna Lane's economy."

My blood was boiling for so many reasons, but I didn't have time to dwell on them right now. With a silent apology to everyone I'd ever paid bills to in town, I tucked the notes back into my pouch. If by some miracle I survived this, I'd have someone take them out of town and evaluate their worth—I still wasn't sure she wasn't lying and these weren't just useless pieces of paper.

"Bank of Ireland?" I asked.

Eithne's Irish brogue became more pronounced. "It's where my mother found my father many centuries back. I spent some time there with his family before moving to Luna Lane—moving far beyond my mother's reach, letting only my little sister know where to find me."

Mom's gaze locked on the floor again.

Our mother. "Bette" and the Poplar family crest. *Eithne Poplar!* Milton had called her that. I'd assumed he'd just been mixed up.

"Eithne is my aunt," I said simply.

"We have different fathers." Mom took a deep breath, though she shouldn't have had need of such a thing. "But in our society, we take our mother's name."

Eithne put a hand on her hip and stared to the side, away from me, refusing to meet my eyes.

"Allaway?" I asked.

"My father's name. I should have taken it years ago, but once we decided on our course of action, your mother and I thought if my last name was the same as yours, you would ask too many questions." Eithne still wouldn't look at me—only my mom.

"It was never Eithne who cursed you," Mom said to me. "She may have always... *had a penchant* for the more *mischievous* side of enchantments than I did, but she was never as cruel as other witches. She was the only one I could trust to keep me—to keep you—safe."

"The curse was always in my blood," I said simply.

"Not a curse," snapped Eithne. "You don't *realize* how bad a curse can be."

"Eithne," said Mom softly. She looked like she wanted to reach out to her *sister*, but she held back her ghostly hand, perhaps too keenly aware of the disappointment if she tried. Mom's eyebrows drew together as she turned back to me. "I worried something like this would happen—we had no idea what the half-witch child of a golem would be like before you were born."

"Who called Doc Day?" I asked.

Eithne and Mom exchanged a silent conversation with a look.

"I know someone posed as Mayor Abdel to call Doc Day right after I was born. The doctor said the mayor claimed it wasn't him—"

"It was I," said Eithne. "I cast an enchantment

to make sure the both of you were healed of whatever damage the birth may have caused, but I know nothing about the health of infants. I just wanted to make sure you were all right." She spared one glance at me under a heavy-lidded eye.

"I asked her not to call anyone," said Mom, admonishing, but there was a light in her eyes I just couldn't match with what the silver-haired witch beside me deserved. "But my big sister always had a soft spot for me."

"She *killed* you!" I shouted, finally snapping.

Mom shook her head. "It was my time. We risked it all to save you—and if our idea didn't work, and it didn't"—she gestured at her ghostly form—"we knew you needed an enemy. I wanted you to dislike her. To have someone to fight against. We wanted you to be strong," Mom said, in echo of what Eithne herself had just told me. "For what lies ahead."

"*What* lies ahead? The other witches? Why would they come for me—and why particularly *now*?"

Eithne and Mom exchanged a glance, another unspoken conversation between them. Eithne's jaw clenched hard.

Then Mom answered. "We agreed. You'd be safe here until you were thirty—but then we had to let you go. Let you live as you saw fit. But you needed a fighting chance. And I would rather, if you're not up to the task, that you never have to face what awaits you. A swift death would be kinder. Your fate now, I'm afraid, depends entirely on you. Darling, I love you. And I hope you will be strong. But if I'm about to welcome you and Broomhilde to the other side with me, then so be it."

My heart thundered, the clarity sending *danger, danger, danger* signals straight to my brain.

"Goodbye," said Mom softly, her limbs vanishing, Broomhannah's bristles returning to nothingness. "I will see you again someday… Or very soon."

She was gone.

And in her place, Eithne stepped inside the rune circle, lifting her arms straight above her head.

Chapter Eighteen

*T*hunder rumbled out in the early morning dawn—and then a bolt of lightning crashed right through the roof, the light, the crackling, overpowering all of my senses.

Eithne channeled the lightning as if it were merely energy and shifted her arms, sending it straight at me.

Despite *everything* I'd just learned, she was trying to kill me.

No sarcasm, no games now.

The clarity sharpened my senses, moved my feet.

The lightning crackled against the rubber boots I'd created out of my ballet slippers, grounding the energy away from me.

The potion in my veins had had the foresight to warn me about that, encouraging me to transform my shoes.

"Don't just dodge!" shouted Eithne. "Show me what you can do."

Was she kidding? She and my mom… Did my mom expect me to *die* in this fight?

But why?

Broomholly picked up Eithne and the two levitated upward, toward the gaping hole Eithne's lightning had cracked into the roof.

"Show me you're not weak!" she said.

Despite the nagging feeling in the back of my head, like this wasn't the best way forward, I struck both my arms out, my left arm still heavy. "ERIF!" I shouted as a torrent of flames burst forth through my fingers.

The power-boosting potion I'd taken earlier, the potion for clarity, my hat, grounding the magical energy from ley lines all around me—whatever it was—came together and more fire than I'd thought possible shot up from my hands.

But Eithne simply flicked her fingers and the fire redirected behind her, sizzling across the early morning light and into the lake water.

Though not before catching the walls of the cabin on fire.

"Disappointing," Eithne said, riding off through the hole in the roof, the cabin fading and the flames extinguishing as it retreated back to ruins.

I flung open the cabin door before it vanished, stepping through, only to find there was no longer a doorway.

Eithne hovered over the stone circle around where a campfire had once been.

"If you can't defeat me, you'll never have a chance against other witches," she said simply.

I clutched my hands into fists. "Is that what this was about? Making me stronger to fight other witches?"

"If any of them find you, they'll come for you," she said. "Why do you think you were confined to this small, out-of-the-way town your whole life?"

My blood ran cold. It hadn't been *part* of my curse—my genetics, whatever? Eithne had indeed trapped me here, but for reasons I'd never imagined?

"You were witch princesses!" I shouted.

"By coven law, so are you," she snapped back.

"I…" I really was a princess? *That aside.* "Why would other witches want to kill me, the daughter of royalty?" I wasn't going to call myself royal just yet.

"It is *because* of who you are that they would see you dead!" Eithne murmured under her breath, lending even more magical energy to enchantments she so rarely needed to do more than think to cast, and the water in the lake behind her started raising in echo of her arms, which she lifted over her head.

She was about to slam the water at me, send it flooding into the campground and rushing into the forest behind me.

"And you would rather I *die* than leave this town?" I shouted. "Than face these other witches?"

Tears gathered at the corners of my eyes. With a startling clarity, my gaze was drawn to the remainder of the water left in the lake, to the glint of black onyx and the shimmer of magical energy.

It was a dome of some kind, and though I could only just make out his head—thank goodness he was so tall—I could see that within that energy bubble was Cable, his eyes closed, his head lolled, but standing up.

Put in some kind of stasis—and kept *under the water* all this time!

"If you knew what our kind was capable of, you would wish the same!" Eithne let loose the water, and three things happened.

I was overcome with a sensation of dread, a desire to run—to where, there seemed to be no option.

Second, the clarity in my veins, weakening somewhat—who knew how long the potion would last—told me the only way out of this now was to fight her and win, and the key lay in the bottom of the lake along with my friends.

And third, I had a sense of how to get there, a clue from Ginny hopping around town during the escape room tragedy, from the clue I'd uncovered about "Bette" vanishing from the coroner's table.

I'd never successfully performed this enchantment before, but I would today.

I had to.

"TROPELET!" I said, holding both my palms toward my own body.

I may not have been able to complete enchantments without relying on words, and I may not have had the most finesse, but right now, I had the willpower—and all the practice I'd done casting stronger and stronger enchantments over the past few months would pay off.

I felt my self *pop*, no longer where I once was. Quickly, on instinct, I redirected myself to where I'd seen Cable.

With a splash, I fell into the water, reappearing in existence from wherever I'd been before I'd even realized.

The flood of the water Eithne had held out into the forest around us echoed wildly in my ears, but I was more focused now on staying afloat.

I realized with a start I'd never exactly swam before.

All of "Bette's" talk of Salem popped in my mind then, the clarity still doing its job. Weren't witches supposed to float?

Forcing the tension out from my muscles, I relaxed, my fingers grazing something smooth and cold.

I took hold of it to anchor me.

It was the pike, stuck down into the lakebed, point end down.

I wasn't sure how long I stayed there, floating, gripping that pike as if it were an anchor, trying to clear my head and listen to the fading inner voice inside of me.

But sometime after the rumble of the spilling water, the creaking trees bending in its wake, had faded, there was a set of piercing howls on the horizon that snapped me back to the moment.

The werewolves? Impossible. Who had freed them? Had Faine gone home—and retrieved her family? She wouldn't put them in danger like that.

Not for me.

I knew I would have for her, but it wasn't the same.

I was alone. I didn't have a spouse or kids. I didn't even have family.

But whatever could explain it, Eithne let out a hiss and I bolted straight up, sending my stiff legs lower into the lake, clutching the pike with both hands to steady me.

Eithne whirled around and laughed. "Clever. Here I was, soaring over the woods to search for you —or what was left of you. Teleportation?" Perhaps she hadn't heard over the roar of her enchantment. Perhaps she hadn't expected it—of me.

I grimaced, the brim of my soggy hat drooping over my eyes. "You taught me that was possible when you helped Ginny kill a man."

"See? It was all educational, wasn't it?" Eithne laughed. What a way to view murder, even if the victim had been a murderer himself. Eithne's view of humankind was warped, to say the least.

"If you were so keen to have me learn how to fight a witch, you should have just stuck around and taught me, *Auntie*." Auntie. *Auntie!* It was she who'd brought me over to Milton's to sing? But no one had ever told me that. *Of course.* Eithne was a master at manipulating memories. She'd made everyone in Luna Lane at the time forget she'd ever been a part of my life. Maybe Milton's dementia was weakening the effects of her magic on him.

My words seemed to have an effect on Eithne, whose brow furrowed.

I turned toward Cable, looking beyond him to find three more magical energy fields just poking above the lowered waters, the other three missing people trapped inside. Relief flooded through me.

"Have you hurt them?" I demanded to know.

"Not yet." Eithne smiled. "If I did, would that help you fight?"

If Mom and Eithne had planned this—despite the fact that Mom *seemed* to have cared for me— then witches really were dark at heart.

I found Broomie's magical energy bubble. She'd be the only one I felt safe waking up in the middle of a lake while my attention was drawn in all different directions just now.

"ESAELER!" I said, focusing on both Broomie's bubble and the pike in my hand.

There was a *pop* and the energy surrounding Broomie fizzled out as if electrocuted. She didn't need even a moment to collect her thoughts because she shot out like a horse at the derby, soaring not right at me, but under the water as I raised the pike above my head.

"Broomie?" I called back, lapping, my feet only just able to graze the bottom. My boots felt heavy under the water. My chin went under, and it strained my neck to just keep my nose above.

But still, my sense of clarity wanted me to hold on to this pike.

Why?

With a splash, Broomie shot back up out of the water.

"Oh, no, you don't." Eithne shot lightning bolts her way.

I shrieked, the water spilling inside my mouth, but I had to help her.

"TCELFED!" I sputtered, raising the pike like a channeling rod.

A moment after, I went under. Staring at the sleeping Cable in front of me, I rested my free hand across the surface of the magical energy surrounding him to say goodbye. But the thudding echo of someone joining me drew my attention. Broomie shot forward, unharmed, dragging the staff I'd created out of the candy bar tightly in her brush. Her handle shot between my legs, and up we rode out from the water and into the sky.

Instead of finding Eithne with her arms aimed right at us, I saw her with her back to us, the werewolves I recognized as Faine and Grady skidding to a stop at the water's edge.

They growled, bearing their maws menacingly —more menacingly than I'd thought either gentle soul capable of.

Behind them, still many paces lagging, there were people trailing after them, the branches swaying as they approached.

I floated with Broomie a moment, my limbs heavy with fatigue, my gut roiling as so many citizens of Luna Lane broke through the treeline.

Sherriff Roan. Mayor Abdel and Chione—even Erik and Ryan, who worked with them at town hall. Jamie and Doc Day. Spindra. Jeremiah and Arjun. I couldn't stay there and count them all.

Their loved ones were missing, and they'd come to find them—but they were *all* now in danger.

"Do you know a witch's weakness?"

Bette's taunting words came back to me. Eithne. It had been Eithne revealing more than I'd even realized.

"Burning witches, seeing if they floated—humans had no idea how to really kill a witch," even Ingrid had said. She'd been repeating Bette's words then, too.

Clarity struck me.

You kill a witch with kindness—not with good deeds and smiles, but to make her save another out of nothing but the kindness of her heart. A witch's weakness came about from her valuing her own life less than someone else's.

Eithne cackled then looked at me over her shoulder, as if she'd always known I'd hovered behind her, the onyx pike held aloft in my stone hand. "So many came to see the show, huh?"

She lifted a hand in their direction, her eyes locked on me.

"Eithne, don't do this!" The small bits of flesh that remained on my left hand sweated under the weight of the cold onyx in my hand and what the last fleeting bit of clarity told me I would have to do. "If you and my mom were beloved sisters—if you really only cursed me to stay in this town and it was all to protect me... It doesn't have to end this way."

The corner of Eithne's full lips twitched up just slightly. "Oh, but it has to end in tragedy either way, sweet little fiery thing."

She flung her hand out, the magic energy brightening on the tips of her fingers, the growing crowd shirking back, screaming.

Could I end this some other way?

Could she still be reasoned with?

No. She'd led me to this weapon. She wanted me to end her. I didn't want to give her what she wanted. I didn't want to taint my soul because this witch was forcing my hand. She would always have wicked blood in her veins—just as I now would—but the cost of not ending this here, now, was too much to bear.

My hand gripped the pike tightly.

"You must," she said, as if reading the thoughts that had popped into my head.

"I... I can't. Don't make me." My voice cracked.

"The others will not hesitate," she said. "*Princess*." The crackle of lightning reflected in her violet eyes, making her look mad. "So no longer shall I dillydally. Do... Or they die!"

She was going to kill them all. It wasn't a bluff, a ploy to trick me into doing what she wanted me to do. The last of the clarity surged through me. My friends were absolutely in danger. She'd get what she wanted from me, all right—or *we all* would be the ones to suffer the consequences.

With a cry and tears flooding my wind-whipped cheeks, I soared forward on Broomie. With the staff still clutched in her bristles, she made a sharp turn as we approached Eithne and Broomholly, whacking the black broomstick so hard with the staff, Broomholly cracked in two. Eithne slipped, her hand shooting its lightning up instead of down at my friends, just as I aimed the pike straight at her chest.

Chapter Nineteen

*E*ithne's body lit up as the pike pierced her, growing bright white with the dispersed power of her lightning spell. Below, Broomholly fell, black splinters spreading out over the lake's waters, her form floating, lifeless and still.

Eithne flailed at the edge of my weapon, my stone arm somehow strong enough to handle the weight of both the weapon and her body on the end of it as we floated, suspended in the air on top of Broomie.

Broomie whimpered beneath me, letting go of the staff. It fell below us with a splash.

With a crackle and a series of pops, the three energy fields hiding the sleeping humans in the water vanished, and the townspeople on the shore leaped into action, wading into the water, the were-wolves going first, their dog legs paddling.

To my relief, Cable, Ingrid, and Goldie acclimated quickly, managing to swim toward the horde headed their way.

They were safe. At last. And everyone was here to save them. I fought down my instinct to use magic to go rescue them.

Because I wasn't done with Eithne yet.

A trickle of blood dripped down her lip and she turned her head my way.

"HTGNERTS," she said softly, gesturing at herself. She was casting an enchantment on herself —not to heal her wounds, but to gather enough strength. For what? To taunt me about how she'd goaded me?

I wouldn't let her. My arms shaking, I opened my mouth to heal her, pulling on what little energy I had left.

"*Don't,*" she snapped. "Don't be such a fool. Just listen. NETSIL." Her word forced me to be still, to listen to her speak. The short window I had to heal her was closing.

If she wanted to be healed, she could do it herself.

But she refused. She coughed, the sound choking and gurgling. "I would never have killed your mother," she said gentler now. "For most of my life—she was the only witch I ever loved. The sweetest, kindest witch who ever was."

"I believe you," I said, not even realizing that would be my answer until it was. "Mom said you two risked it all?"

"The para-paranormal…" she started.

"You knew about it from your dealings with Ravana—and whoever else," I guessed. She didn't respond, so I figured I'd gotten it right. "And Mom… Mom thought perhaps it would take my powers away, keep me from being a witch or maybe a gargoyle?"

As if to punctuate my theory—though there was no para-paranormal present that I felt; it was more like the fading of Eithne meant her magic was fading, too—below me, the two werewolves yelped, their fur shedding, their limbs elongated and becoming human, just as they met up with the three humans who'd been kept captive under the water.

"I didn't want to try it," she said. "I knew it was dangerous. And I didn't want you to be a normie to be safe. But we had no other options. She was willing to die… To try."

I choked back the tears forming. Mom had *known* she would likely die to produce the para-paranormal? The two paranormal presences had really just been her and Eithne, the death my mom's own?

But why? Had she loved me that much?

"It didn't work," croaked Eithne. "Two witches, one death, but there have to be at least three people involved in its creation. Two to cast dark magic, a third to die. I suspected as much, based on what the other members of our coven had done before, but Cinnamon would not risk harming a single soul besides her own. The stuff wasn't potent. If I'd known Ravana's and my dark energy had created some in the Woodwards' attic already by then, we wouldn't have needed to try to create some of our own at all." A single tear fell down her cheek. "But it was such a weak substance at that point, I couldn't even sense it until it became stronger with Leana's murder in the attic all those years later. And then, despite all of that, the sacrifice might not have been in vain if it had worked. But even when you were exposed to the real version of the stuff, your witch powers faded, and never your stone scales." She clutched at my stone arm with a weak grip.

"She died for nothing," Eithne said sadly. "But it was our last hope. We didn't know what else to do to save you from turning to stone." She smiled wistfully.

"And you?" I said, my own voice cracking. "Are you dying for nothing?" I was crying now. For Eithne.

"I'm dying for you." The color retreated from her rosy flesh.

"But why? How would this help?" My voice rose in pitch. "You made me... You *tainted* me by leading me to kill you. By not letting me heal you."

"Because Cinnamon is my sister, and I love you." Eithne's voice was waning. "And now I know... When driven to protect those you love, you'll do what you must do. You'll defeat any witch who comes your way. Just don't... Don't be foolish enough to heal them." She looked down at the pike still sticking out of her chest. "You know what can kill a witch now. Your father's onyx pike I transformed into all those cards is part of it—the Poplar crest includes it as a flaunting mockery of the weapon that can bring down the witch royal house —but there's the other component as well. Love is a witch's weakness—her real strength, too. And no other witch realizes how powerful love is."

Salty tears settled on my lips. "But you do." Of all the things I'd ever thought I'd say to Eithne, that had not been one. "*You* understand love."

"Be free, my love." She closed her eyes, the smile lightning up her face before her head rolled back, her limbs growing limp.

"Are you sure about this?" Roan asked.

Most of the citizens who'd come to my rescue had followed behind me, the doctor and Arjun staying with Ingrid and Goldie to make sure they warmed up by the fire I'd started for them at the campsite. I'd dried them all—Cable, too—but they were all right. I believed they just needed some quiet, some warmth, some time to acclimate to what had happened.

Cable told me it had felt like a dream, but a nightmare, too—as if he'd been hopelessly, endlessly drowning.

"I have to know," I said, clutching Broomie by

the shaft in one hand, swallowing back the lump in my throat that had stuck there since Eithne had passed on.

At the edge of the lake, Spindra wove silk threads between her hands, her usually-perfect skin somewhat yellowed, her head bobbing every few seconds, like she was fighting off exhaustion from a lack of sleep. She was mostly nocturnal, but since she'd helped with the search yesterday, she was long overdue for a rest. Now, she was expending what little energy she had to weave a soft, silk shroud with which to cover Eithne before she could be taken to the local funeral home.

The bits of Broomholly that I could gather with my enchantment lay on top of the shroud, the black wooden splinters and loose bristles contrasting sharply with the white silk. I watched as the toes of Eithne's slippers, the last part of her left exposed, were covered by Spindra's silk, line by line.

Farewell, my aunt.

Before I took a step forward past the farthest place I'd ever been outside of Luna Lane, someone grabbed my stone hand, the cold, stone scales there unable to absorb the warmth of the firm squeeze.

I whirled and Cable smiled down at me. "If what you told us is true, what if you stepping foot outside of town alerts these other witches to your presence?"

I'd told them everything—well, almost everything. I'd left out the part about the three of us Luna Lane witches being lost princesses.

It was just too embarrassing to think about.

I swallowed. Now that I knew that despite her supporting role in several murders, Eithne had been the *mild* kind of mischievous witch, that the others *truly* wanted me dead—no games, no toying with me, they'd strike me down before I could blink—I was frightened.

Scared to achieve something I'd wanted for all my days.

Freedom. Not to turn my back forever on the place I called home, but to explore, to grow, to maybe come back, but only after knowing it was where I truly wanted to be.

"Either way, if the enchantment keeping me here broke with Eithne's death like those other enchantments of hers, they'll find me."

I squeezed his hand back, being careful not to put too much pressure on the grip.

He let me go.

Broomie and I took one step forward, and I followed that with a deep breath.

The bent branch on the old, scarred tree to the right of me.

The moss-covered stone to the left.

"The barrier keeping me in is—*was*—just here," I announced to everyone. "Just a few steps in front of me." I could have heard a pine needle falling to the soft, mossy ground just then.

I didn't reach my hand out this time. It was going to work. And if it didn't, I had to know. I stepped forward, past the markers.

My boot hit ground on the other side, nothing stopping me.

Behind me, the crowd let out a little cry of joy.

I whirled around, blinking. "Are you *that* excited to see me go?"

"No, silly!" Faine darted forward, the chic leaf-pattern dress I'd managed to enchant her out of literal dead leaves swishing around her. When she and Grady had turned back to humans, they hadn't had any clothes on, so I'd made Grady a set of leaf overalls, too. My best friend embraced me, then pulled back. "We're happy for you, of course! We love you. Why do you think we all came to save you?"

My mouth gaped open as I took in the sight of those around me.

They'd come for me—not just Goldie, Ingrid, and Cable?

Of course they had. I'd been so focused on saving those three, had even accepted I might not make it back, it hadn't occurred to me that other people would have fought just as hard to save me, too.

I wanted to chastise her for risking her safety—to chastise *everyone*—but instead, crying just a little, I hugged her again. She returned the embrace and nudged me as she stepped back. "Besides, you

237

belong in Luna Lane. We know you'd never leave us for good."

I'd never leave them for good? Even if I could?

Somehow, though I'd never given it much thought—I'd almost never really thought this day would come—I knew she was right.

I would enjoy my freedom, but I would always come home.

My eyes darted guiltily to Cable. But Cable wouldn't always be here to come home to.

Still, now I could visit him. And… And…

My heart sunk. I didn't know what I wanted now. Before, when my future had been closed and my heart about to break, it had almost been simpler.

I'd had no choice but to let him go.

Now, I'd let go of something, and it would hurt me somehow—but it would be all *me*. I would be the one to decide, and freedom now seemed a heavy burden.

"Talk about something to be thankful for!" shouted Faine, raising my stone arm along with her flesh one above us. Broomie slipped from my fingers to float around her and rub her and me both repeatedly with her brush like a flying, scenting cat. We both laughed. "Dinner may not be as grand as it usually is, but we still have quite a few hours before the sun sets. I say we all head back and enjoy Thanksgiving—as the whole town of Luna Lane!"

Everyone cheered and turned, a few making their way to me to offer their congratulations.

Spindra shook her head to shift her black hair over one eye and looked amusingly between Cable and me, leaning over to whisper, "I say the first thing you do is join that handsome professor for his upcoming trip. Either that, or I can have him *over for dinner* sometime." She cackled, amused.

I winced, but I couldn't stop the smile from reaching my lips when I realized Cable had heard it all.

Broomie floated overhead as Cable took my hands in his.

"Would you like to?"

"Would I like to what?" I teased. He was going to have to ask me outright.

"Join me on my sabbatical trip? I should only be gone a couple of weeks."

Broomie moaned, shaking her bristles, as the retreating footfalls of the townsfolk headed back toward town grew fainter and fainter.

"That depends," I said. Broomie shook wildly, her handle flicking back and forth in evident anger.

"On what?" Cable's gaze kept flicking above us.

"Do you have room in that tiny car of yours for a broomstick who'll do her best to stay still when other people are around?"

Broomie stiffened, her brush turning slightly to Cable, as if waiting for his answer with bated breath.

"*That* depends," he said.

Broomie shook her bristles quickly again.

"On?"

"If she can promise to stop scaring the living daylights out of me."

Broomie tittered and soared around us both, accidentally—or intentionally—slamming us chest-to-chest.

The brim of my hat knocked his glasses and I bent the hat backward while he fixed his spectacles, but then Broomie kept shoving us closer together.

We both laughed nervously, then turned our heads at the same time, our lips only centimeters apart.

I rose up on my toes just slightly and kissed him.

He grabbed me by the back and squeezed me tightly, his mouth soft and firm and practically *craving* my own.

With a screech, I pulled back, my left arm tingling.

"What's wrong?" Cable asked, pulling back as his gaze flitted all over me—settling on my left arm.

I held up my arm, ignoring the murmurings from the crowd likely headed back in my direction at my shout as I watched my silver skin turn a cool rosy cream, the stone scales retreating everywhere to be replaced by flesh.

"What?" Cable blinked hard. "How?"

Eithne's throwaway line burst into my mind. "No," I whispered. Had she really known? Or had she just been teasing me? Perhaps I'd never know.

Then louder, I said, "True love's kiss. That's how to keep the stone at bay."

"That's amazing! I'm so happy for—" Cable cut himself short and did a double-take. "*True love?*"

Turning, I patted him on the chest, putting more distance between us. "Sorry, it's nothing. I shouldn't have said—"

But he grabbed me again and gave me another kiss.

"Dahlia?" Faine asked, though her tone broke from anxiety to amusement. "Are you all right?" She gasped.

Before I could answer, Broomie rushed between Cable's and my legs as one. Cable let out a little yelp, though I was the one riding backward. I gripped on to him, steadying him, as my companion broomstick took us off into the bright blue sky.

He swallowed, looking down.

"Hold on to me, handsome," I said, giving him another quick kiss. "I won't let you fall."

That was all it took for him to latch on to me and give in as we dotted the sky with our silhouettes, my lips on his all the while.

Join the Spooky Games Club in Curses and Crosswords

Free of her curse, Luna Lane's resident witch, Dahlia Poplar, sets foot outside of her paranormal small town for the first time in her life. Accompanying her new professor boyfriend on a tour of literature sites across the country, she expands her horizons while trying harder than ever to keep her powers under wraps—and prevent her magic broomstick from revealing their supernatural natures.

Just as they're about to head home, their car breaks down and they decide to take the train back to Luna Lane to join friends and family in time for the holidays. This two-day, one-night journey includes a crossword puzzle event to entertain the passengers. As two founding members of the latest iteration of Spooky Games Club, Dahlia and her boyfriend are excited to take part—until they realize there's something sinister going on.

Before the train ride ends, a crossword champion is acting strange, and Dahlia suspects a curse is at play. Belongings go missing, a mysterious villain threatens murder, and the train is unable to stop or slow down. Dahlia realizes she isn't the only paranormal presence on board—and if she wants to make it home again, she'll have to unscramble the clues across and down to solve the puzzle before it's too late.

Witchy Expo Services Mysteries:
Magic, Conventions, and Murder

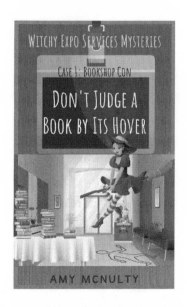

Witchy Expo Services. We host your convention, expo, or trade show—with a dash of magic!

Set up in a matter of days, our expos can host even the largest of crowds in our witch-run village of Cauldron Cove. We can offer what no other expo planners can: breathtaking illusions, instant teleportation from one end of the center to the other, floating item storage, and all the exceptional, magical touches that will make your event one-of-a-kind. Inquire about Cauldron Cove hosting your next event today by contacting Bernadette Toothaker, award-winning Head Witch General Manager of Witchy Expo Services for eleven decades.

Nimue Toothaker is ecstatic that her world-famous grandmother is about to retire and has chosen her as her successor in the family business. She's only been working on the expos for a few years, but she's confident she has what it takes to lead her fellow witches and warlocks in the business that defines their entire village. Unfortunately, her grandmother's sole condition for Nimue taking the job is that she share the position with her arch rival, an irritating warlock possessed of two minds—quite literally.

First up is Bookshop Con, where indie booksellers from across the nation host authors and sell books to passionate readers. Nimue's grand plans clash with her co-manager's persnickety demands, but their arguments cease to matter when a celebrated author drops dead in the convention center lobby. Nimue suspects murder, but she knows that if she ends the convention prematurely, the magic at work will destroy her beloved hometown. It's a race to catch the killer before they strike again—all while trying to prove she can handle the job she's so desperately always wanted.

About the Author

Amy McNulty is an editor and author of books that run the gamut from YA speculative fiction to contemporary romance. A lifelong fiction fanatic, she fangirls over books, anime, manga, comics, movies, games, and TV shows from her home state of Wisconsin. When not reviewing anime professionally or editing her clients' novels, she's busy fulfilling her dream by crafting fantastical worlds of her own.

Sign up for Amy's newsletter to receive news and exclusive information about her current and upcoming projects. Get a free YA romantic sci-fi novelette when you do!

Find her at amymcnulty.com and follow her on social media:

amazon.com/author/amymcnulty

bookbub.com/authors/amy-mcnulty

facebook.com/AmyMcNultyAuthor

twitter.com/mcnultyamy

instagram.com/mcnulty.amy

pinterest.com/authoramymc

Look for More Reads from Crimson
Fox Publishing

Crimson Fox
PUBLISHING

Bag of Tricks

CARMEN WEBSTER BUXTON

Aveline is a trained magician, but Princess Inessa, the Heiress of Mazuria, hired her to pose as a lady-in-waiting, to protect her from court intrigues and literally sniff out lies. When a wicked duke tries to force Inessa into marriage, Aveline uses a spell to hide the princess. But even magic has limits, and when Aveline stumbles over Zarek, a man whose life has been cursed by more than one tragedy, she demands his help in getting the princess back to the capital. Zarek is on his own errand, and he's suspicious of Aveline—magicians are feared—but he does help. As he and Aveline travel Mazuria in company with the princess and his wolf-dog Burden, they come to rely on each other and to respect each other's skills. After Zarek leaves the two women in what he thinks is a safe refuge, he learns they're in more danger than ever. So of course he and Burden go back to save them.

Now if only Aveline can bring herself to believe that Zarek wants to save her even more than he wants to save the princess—and admit to herself that what she feels for him goes way beyond gratitude.

The Heart of Doctor Steele

COLETTE DIXON

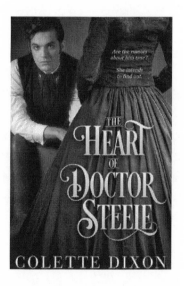

Are the rumors about him true? She intends to find out.

The mysterious Dr. Steele has taken up residence next door, and scandalous rumors about him are spreading through Margaret Landeau's small Massachusetts town. Rumors of women he's ill-used and exploited for his experimental surgeries. Never one to believe gossip, Margaret arms herself with a basket of baked goods and ventures to discover the truth from the man himself.

John Steele has lost everything. His parents, his aunt, too many women he intended to save, and his good name. All he has left is his aunt's home in a far-flung village and a library he's stocked with whiskey. He has nothing to offer anyone. Especially not the bold woman next door whose passion for healing reminds him of the man he once was.

But when a dangerously ill girl arrives on his doorstep, pleading for help, Margaret is thrust into his world. She will learn who the real Dr. John Steele truly is, and soon, not even his dark past can stop her from fighting for the brilliant doctor she now loves. But he must deny his crushing desire for her—loving a man like him can only cast a shadow over her own bright future.

Made in the USA
Middletown, DE
26 February 2023